Morning in a Different Place

Morning in a Different Place

Mary Ann McGuigan

FRONT STREET
Honesdale, Pennsylvania

ACKNOWLEDGMENTS
Thanks so much to Joy Neaves, a gifted editor, for her scrupulous care
and excellent suggestions; to George Nicholson for pointing the way in
the long search to find *Morning* a home; to David Colin for his brilliant
plot solution; to fellow scribbler Mary Rowland for cheering me on
when the effort seemed pointless; and to Matt and Doug, who show me
again and again what's most important.

Lyrics from "We Want No Irish Here" by Tommy Makem
reprinted here with permission of Conor Makem.

LIBRARY OF CONGRESS CATALOGING-IN-PUBLICATION DATA
McGuigan, Mary Ann.
Morning in a different place / Mary Ann McGuigan. — 1st ed.
p. cm.
Summary: In 1963 in the Bronx, New York, eighth-graders Fiona and
Yolanda help one another face hard decisions at home despite family and
social opposition to their interracial friendship, but Fiona is on her own
when popular classmates start paying attention to her and give her a glimpse
of both a different way of life and a new kind of hatefulness.
ISBN-13: 978-1-59078-551-5 (hardcover : alk. paper)
[1. Friendship—Fiction. 2. Race relations—Fiction. 3. Family
problems—Fiction. 4. Schools—Fiction. 5. African Americans—Fiction.
6. Self-actualization (Psychology)—Fiction. 7. Bronx (New York, N.Y.)—
History—20th century—Fiction.] I. Title.
PZ7.M47856Mor 2008
[Fic]—dc22
2007017547

FRONT STREET
An Imprint of Boyds Mills Press, Inc.
815 Church Street
Honesdale, Pennsylvania 18431

For Alice

1

Now I know what invisible feels like. Yolanda's been in Lexington Hospital for more than two weeks, and I've been walking big as life through its huge, squeaky glass doors, marching along the main hall past the gift shop to the elevator that takes me—no questions asked—to the third floor. No one wants to know where I'm going, who I am. At least two of the orderlies can see me just fine, though, because they smile and give me a nod. The older one is reading the *Daily News* from two days ago: Saturday, October 26, 1963. I've seen it already. There's a picture of the president and Jackie Kennedy again, welcoming Marshal Tito and Mrs. Tito of Yugoslavia to the White House. The younger orderly, the one with the head that shines like a new black bowling ball, is the one who showed me how to find Yolanda's room the first day.

Yolanda's got a broken rib and a dislocated shoulder. Well, not anymore. I mean the shoulder's been relocated, and the whole business sounds a lot worse than it is. In fact, the doctors may not know it yet, but she's fine. She's so fine that she has her escape all planned. It wasn't my idea. I swear. All I did was tell her yesterday that you can walk around this place and nobody gives you a second look. That's when she told me to bring her some clothes to wear. I told her I couldn't do that, that she shouldn't just leave the hospital without permission and go wandering through the Bronx again. She gave me a look, like I should have figured out already that she's got her own rules about what she does.

So here I am with stolen clothes in a paper bag—my cousin Bea's pedal pushers and a pink sweatshirt. Bea is only eleven, but she's about Yolanda's size. Yolanda's small for thirteen, I guess. But really she's almost fourteen, like me. I hope Yolanda won't get mad when she sees that the shirt's pink. She doesn't seem like the girlie type to me, but that's the best I could do. Most of my own clothes are still in storage or at my father's place. My mother and me and my sister, Cait, and my little brother, Owen, are living with my aunt Maggie now. So's my big brother, Liam, at least when he's around. We got evicted from our apartment on Mapes Avenue on October 11, more than two weeks ago, and we couldn't take all our clothes with us. Aunt Maggie's got five kids of her own. So it's a sardine can of a life.

Yolanda's asleep when I get to the room. The white sheet is tucked under her chin, and with her nose in the air and her head so small and dark on the pillowcase, she looks like a chocolate kiss in vanilla ice cream. *American Bandstand* is on the television, the show Yolanda claims she never watches. She says the kids on the show dance like they learned from mannequins on speed and that Dick Clark, the host, is barely a notch cooler than Lawrence Welk, the band leader on Channel 7 that even my mother calls an old fart. Yolanda likes the Temptations and Chuck Berry. She didn't think I liked them, but I do. Liam has their records.

I don't know if it's okay to wake Yolanda, so I put the bag of clothes on the floor and sit down in the chair near the bed. The room is quiet. I can hear the nurses' voices from down the hall and a humming noise from somewhere, maybe the room next door where that old woman is, the one with her bed covered in Saran Wrap. Already I'm getting warm, so I take my coat off. Yolanda isn't snoring, but she's making funny sounds, a nervous breathing that comes and goes. I wonder if she's dreaming. She turns on her side and her arm comes out from under the covers. I'm struck by how dark her skin is, and now I can look as long as I like without her seeing. I hardly ever notice anymore what color she is, so I don't know why it has my attention today. It's just that there is so much that's forbidden about Yolanda. Because she's colored, I'm not supposed to visit her in the hospital, I'm not supposed to want to hang out with her, I'm not supposed to want to be in her house. All the fuss gives her color a life of its own, as if it's something separate from Yolanda herself.

I stand and move closer to the bed. Up close, I see that her eyes are moving, like when Aunt Maggie's dog, Little Feather, is sleeping. I wonder what Yolanda's skin feels like. I turn and look at the doorway to make sure no one's there. I'm not sure it's normal to want to, but I do. I touch her skin, her forearm, the place below her elbow. It's soft. It feels just like mine, just like anybody's. Yolanda opens her eyes and smiles at me.

"Hey, Fiona," she says. "Hi."

I say hi back. I've already taken my hand away, and I don't think she knows what woke her.

"How's it going?" she says.

I tell her okay, but I hate it at my aunt Maggie's house. I spend as much time at the hospital as I can. Aunt Maggie's really nice and all. It's just that you can't pack three grown-ups, eight kids, and one in-betweener—that's Liam—into five rooms and expect the density not to make everybody crazy.

I never thought I'd miss that ugly apartment on Mapes Avenue. I hated it when my mother moved us there. It didn't feel like home at all. A lot of my stuff was still at the apartment where we lived with my dad. And as if sharing a room with Cait wasn't bad enough, Mom had to bunk in with us, too. But it was better than what we have now, which is nothing. Yesterday my cousin Maureen took all her cosmetics from her dresser and put them in a box with a lock on it. Like me or Cait would ever be seen dead in her Tangerine Tango lipstick or her Rose Rush rouge that makes her look like she's just escaped from a doll factory where something went seriously wrong.

"What time is it?" says Yolanda.

"About three thirty."

"How was school?"

I roll my eyes. I'm in yet another new school 'cause Aunt Maggie lives on Bathgate Avenue, about a mile away from Mapes. I missed school for a whole week after we moved in, but finally my mom registered me at the school near there. I started more than a week ago. And once again I don't know anyone, except my cousins, who I don't want to know. The younger ones are okay, but Maureen and Ed hate me. I can't really blame them. Who would want their place turned into a homeless shelter? School is even worse. Being an outsider, not belonging, comes down to such ordinary things. Like when I have to tell teachers how to say my name: Fiona O'Doherty. I wouldn't bother telling them on my own because I don't care how they pronounce it, except that every teacher in every class asks the same thing: did I pronounce that correctly? And they never do, so I have to say it for them, loud enough for everyone to hear, in a room full of suddenly attentive kids who've known each other's names since kindergarten.

"Did you bring the clothes?" Yolanda says.

"In the bag," I tell her.

She wants to see what I brought, so I hand the bag to her. She moans when she sees the color, but she doesn't fuss. I'm still in the skirt I wore to school, so we won't exactly match. "They'll have to do. Give me a second," she says and scoots off the bed, wincing, and into the bathroom with the bag. I look around, but there's not much to see. On her night table are some magazines, a book; some playing cards from a deck have fallen on the floor. I pick them up and put them on the night table with the rest. I notice a large greeting card, tucked between the phone and the water pitcher. The envelope is postmarked South Carolina. I slip the card out and look at it. There's a sunrise on the front, all sentimental. I peek inside and see that it's from Yolanda's mother. There's a long note from her at the end, but the only part I get the chance to read is where she says she'll be there by the end of the week, because Yolanda comes out of the bathroom and sees me reading it.

"I'm sorry," I say. "I ..."

"Just leave it," she says. She's all dressed, with her hair in two short thick braids. She's in a hurry but moving stiffly, and I see that she's still in some pain. She asks again what time it is, and I tell her it's a quarter to four. She says we should go.

"Are you sure this is a good idea?" I ask.

"Yes."

"You look like you're still hurting."

"It's nothing. Anyway, I'm going to hurt just as much if I stay here."

"But you don't know how you're going to feel walking around. At least here you'd be in bed."

"I don't want to be in bed," she says.

"Is it because your mother's coming?" She gives me a look that tells me I shouldn't ask her to explain. It's none of my business, but I hate that she won't tell me. It makes me feel like I'm not important to her. But I don't ask her again. "Where are we going?" I say.

"One thing at a time." She goes to the narrow closet and

takes out the only thing hanging there, a huge sweater that looks like it weighs a ton.

Yolanda walks to the door and peeks out. She holds her finger up to tell me to wait. After a moment, she looks outside again, satisfied this time that it's safe to go. We move quickly and in a matter of seconds we're down the hall and into the stairwell, both of us a little breathless, although we haven't gone very far. The stairwell smells less like ammonia than the hall does. I take a breath and try to calm down. That's when Yolanda looks at me and grins. She seems relieved, as if she's just escaped some awful fate. I think she's about to say something, but the sound of a door opening onto the landing below keeps her quiet. For a second I don't know what we should do, but then the footsteps head away from us to a floor below.

We remain still, waiting for it to get quiet again. Finally, we're sure we're the only ones on the stairs. I want to say something, ask her why we're doing this, but the question hangs on me like a weight. I don't want to pretend anymore. Not with Yolanda. She won't trust me, won't tell me what this is about, why she wants to leave the hospital so badly and without her family's permission. And I don't want to pretend that the secrets are okay.

Yolanda takes a few steps down the stairs and realizes I haven't followed. She turns and looks at me. "Come on," she says, but I don't answer. She looks at me again, suspicious. "What are you standing there for?"

"I want to know why we're doing this."

She turns her back and goes down another few steps, and her words trail carelessly behind her. "It's no big deal," she says. "I just don't need to be here anymore. I'm fine."

She doesn't hear me follow, and when she reaches the landing she turns again. She doesn't like the way I'm looking at her. "What's with you?" she says.

"Nothin'."

"Come on, then."

I shake my head no.

"What's going on?"

"I don't want to be shut out," I tell her. "I want to know why you're doing this." She sighs, the way Cait does when she thinks I'm taking things too personally. But she doesn't answer me. "I don't want to be here if I have to pretend with you, too."

"You don't have to pretend with me."

"So is this about your mother?"

Her body caves in a little, and she slides down the wall and sits on the landing. "Yes," she says. "It's about my mother." She plays with the huge button on her sweater. "She's coming up from South Carolina today." I can barely hear her. "And I'm pretty sure when she goes back, she's planning to take me with her." I come down to the landing and sit beside her. I look at her face, hoping she's kidding around. But she's serious, a little scared at the edges, and the idea of her being gone tightens up my chest. I can't breathe right. I bite my lip and clench my fists so I won't cry or do something stupid.

"Why?" is all I can get out.

"She says things are getting out of hand here."

"'Cause you got hurt?"

"That didn't help."

That part's my fault. I don't say it, but Yolanda reads it on my face. Yolanda got hurt because of Liam. The day we got evicted and Liam and I took off for my dad's place, I didn't know it, but I was carrying a little brown bag around that Liam had stashed in my pocketbook that morning— drugs that he was supposed to deliver. When he didn't, his business partners from the north side of Crotona Park came looking for their stuff.

What neither of us knew then was that I'd wind up running away that day, pocketbook and all. My family couldn't find me, but Liam's friends sure did—at Yolanda's place.

"Forget it," she says. "My mom's the one who's out of hand."

"When did she go down to South Carolina?"

"Back in June. For her health. They said she was going to 'need some rest.'" It's clear from the way Yolanda says it that she doesn't believe what they've told her. Sounds phony to me, too, but I don't say so.

"So that's why you moved in with your aunt Cheryl?"

"Yup."

"How come you didn't transfer to a school near your aunt's house?"

"That was the plan. But I wouldn't go."

"You wouldn't transfer?"

"Nope. I told them I was staying in the same school."

"The same school we went to when you lived near me?"

"Yup."

"But how do you get there every day?"

"I walk."

I shake my head. She's amazing. I almost say it. She won't let grown-ups jerk her around. She makes it sound so simple, but my folks have me so boxed in I can't say "good morning" unless I know they'll agree. My big rebellion was telling my mother I was going to see Yolanda at the hospital. My mother was against it, 'cause Yolanda is colored. But I don't know if that really counts as a rebellion. I mean, I didn't plan it. I just had to do it. Nothing my mother could have done or said could have made me feel worse than not going to see Yolanda. "I wish I had your courage," I mumble.

"What do you call running away from your father's place? Sleeping on a park bench?"

Yolanda's talking about the day I ran away from home. But that's not exactly true. You can't run away from home unless you have one. I went back to my father's apartment, on Bryant Avenue, the place that used to be our home before my mother decided to get us away from my dad to an apartment of our own. She finally got tired of needing sunglasses rain or shine. The apartment she moved us to, the one on Mapes Avenue, was the one we got evicted from, seven months after we moved in. It was no palace, but it beat living ringside. Anyway, when they put our furniture in the street, me and Liam took off for the old homestead, where my father still lives.

"That wasn't courage. It was just the opposite," I tell her. It's hard to say the rest. "I was afraid."

"What?"

"My father was crazy drunk and wiping the floor with Liam. It looked like I was going to be next." I can't look at her while I say this. "I should have tried to help him." Instead I tried to run as far as I could. I couldn't stand how it felt to watch Liam get hit. Liam had figured going back to Dad's was better than standing in the street with the living-room furniture and wondering where we were going to sleep that night. He knew Dad wouldn't be home, and he wasn't. We spent the day scrounging food from the cabinets and listening to Liam's records. But Dad came home mean and drunk and mad at the world. And Liam got the blame. I was so scared I shook all over, and no trick I could do inside my head would block out what I was feeling or what he was doing to Liam. I had to get out. So I ran. I just kept going.

"Don't be stupid," says Yolanda. "What could you have done? I would have done the same thing."

"No, you wouldn't." And I know that for a fact. Because when Liam's friends from that gang came to Yolanda's house looking for their drugs, she stood up to them—and got hurt for it. I didn't tell her how I felt when the boys went for her instead of me, how relieved I was. The shame of it makes me sick. I can't stand thinking about any of this. "Why does it have to be South Carolina anyway?" I ask her. "Why did she have to go all the way down there to rest?"

"'Cause that's where her new man went."

I don't say anything. We get up and walk down the stairs as quietly as we can and get down to the first-floor landing. I reach for the door handle, but Yolanda puts her hand on mine and stops me from opening it. "I was going to tell you about my mother, Fiona. I planned on telling you all along."

I nod, grateful. The words feel like a sip of something sweet.

"Telling is just hard," Yolanda says.

I understand how hard it is. She knows I do. The morning after I ran away, the morning after I slept on that bench, I wandered around the streets, heading nowhere, until I ran into Yolanda, and it was as if she'd been waiting for me—there on her crooked front porch. She took me into her house, asked me if I was okay. I wasn't. And she wouldn't let me pretend that I was. So I told her what happened. And once I did, something changed, something about who I was. I was still Fiona, the girl whose living-room furniture was sitting out on the street. But now I had someone, someone who knew what happened and wanted to be with me anyway.

I motion Yolanda to follow me as I walk real casual down the hall toward the sunshine in the lobby. I've never seen so many people in the hospital lobby before. I guess more people visit late in the afternoon, but the crowd makes it even less likely we'll be noticed. No one seems to see us. One man following his wife across the lobby gives me a nasty look, but I think it's because I'm with a Negro girl, not because he suspects anything. He's gray-haired and hard-edged and walks as if his huge size is some kind of accomplishment. I look away. We're just a few steps from the double doors, just a moment away from pulling off our escape, when I feel a hand grasp my shoulder.

"Young lady," I hear someone say. My stomach tightens. I turn around to see who it is. A middle-aged blond woman is standing there, looking rushed and upset. "I need your help," she says. Worry creases frame her eyes and her mouth, but she's still pretty in spite of them. "Can you help me?"

I look at her, confused.

"I just need someone to watch the dog." She's got a long, blue silky scarf around her neck, and she's pulling at it in a nervous way that makes her seem even more upset.

"The dog?"

"Yes, my son has her outside, but he needs to come upstairs with me. It's important." She looks at me as if I should understand all this by now, as if I'm not a stranger but someone who knows all about what's happened and would surely want to help.

"But …"

"It's my mother." Her voice catches at the word. "He needs to see my mother."

And I see more clearly now the kind of upset she is. Her lip is trembling, and something in her eyes makes her look like she's been told to prepare for awful news. I look at Yolanda. She nods, and we follow the woman outside. A tall, lanky kid is standing by the curb, one hand deep in his jacket pocket, the other holding the end of a dog's leash. The dog gets excited as soon as it spots the woman, and twists the leash around a parking meter.

"Dusty, stop," the boy yells. His voice cracks and I look at him more closely. He's only about fifteen. His height made me think he was older.

"Here, David. I'll get her." As soon as she says his name, I realize I know this boy. It's David Silverman. He went to our school last year. He was in the eighth grade. But he's gotten so much older-looking and so much taller. The woman takes the leash and coaxes the dog gently to her. David looks at me and Yolanda. His pale eyes don't trust us, and he doesn't want us to look at him. But I can't help it. His nose is too big, and there's something too shadowy about his upper lip, as if he hasn't washed. Or maybe he needs to shave but his skin is too soft for a razor. Shaving would hurt with those pimples on his chin. He looks a little angry, but it's not because of us. He doesn't want to be here.

"The girls are going to watch Dusty for us," the woman tells him, then turns around and smiles at me. She's grateful. This small favor has eased things for her in a way she can't explain.

"You said I didn't have to go up," David says to his mother as if she's gone back on some solemn promise.

She doesn't answer him. She talks to me instead. "We won't be long," she says. "She's a good dog."

I nod. She's certainly a friendly one. No sooner does the woman hand me the leash than Dusty begins her investigation, sniffing as many parts as she can reach. By the time she finishes with me and moves on to Yolanda, David and his mom are through the glass doors. He stays several steps behind her, slouching as if he's being dragged back to the scene of some terrible failure. But soon they're too far into the lobby for me to see them anymore.

"Wonder what's eating him," says Yolanda.

"Can't be much fun having to go watch you grandmother make her big exit." I hold the leash tighter. The dog is restless and big, a golden retriever.

"You think she's going to die?"

"Didn't you see the look on the woman's face? Whatever's happening, it can't be good."

Yolanda strokes Dusty's head, but it doesn't keep her still for long. The dog turns to see if I have something better to offer. Unfortunately, neither of us has anything to give her to eat. In fact, I hardly ate any lunch. It was a cold meatloaf sandwich, most of which I gave to the kid sitting across from me, the one with the bits of lettuce in his teeth who always wears the same blue-striped shirt.

"How long do you think they'll be?" says Yolanda. She's eager to go. Maybe she's afraid someone from her family will come along and find us here. She and the dog make a good pair, shifting from one spot to another, on the lookout for anything that might come along.

I shrug but tell her it probably won't be long. And it probably won't, 'cause David is sure to start giving his mother a hard time.

We watch the people come in and out of the glass doors. A lot of them stop and look around once they get a few steps outside, and they look like they're glad to be out of there but ashamed to be so glad. The man always takes the woman's elbow, even though you can tell it's mostly the men who need something to hold on to.

"So what's next?" I say.

"What do you mean?"

"I mean when we get finished here. Where are we going?"

"Got any ideas?"

"Ideas?" I say. "You're the one who wanted to do this,

remember?" One thing is clear, anyway: neither one of us wants to go home. I'm not sure what's waiting for Yolanda, but if I can put off squeezing myself back into my aunt's cattle car of an apartment, that's fine with me. The air in the place is thick with things people can't say. And nothing belongs to me, not even a corner's worth of space. When I put my schoolbag down after school, there's no place I can put it that isn't meant for something else.

"We could go hang out at your dad's for a while."

I give her a look, thinking she must be joking. There's already been enough trouble there.

"Where did you tell your mom you were going to be today?" Yolanda asks.

I don't have an answer.

"You didn't tell her you'd be late comin' home?"

"Well, she knows I visit you at the hospital. I mean, we don't talk about it, but she knows."

"Why don't you talk about it?"

"It's nothin'."

"It's something. What?"

There's a second or two of silence.

"She doesn't want me coming here."

"Why?" Yolanda says. She knows why, but for some mean reason she wants to hear me say it.

I never meant for us to get into this, about my mother not wanting me to be friends with a colored girl, so I tell her something else. "It's too far. She doesn't like me riding on buses and all."

"Look at me," Yolanda says, but I don't. "You're lying."

I don't know what to say, so we just watch the doors for another long while, and she must be able to see as plain as I can that when people come out in pairs, they're always the same color. That's just the way it is. I'm not saying it's right, but it's a fact. Whites don't hang around with Negroes just to be friends. Only if there's a good reason, like work or business. I hate it 'cause it makes me feel like something's wrong with the way I feel about Yolanda. She's the only thing in my life right now that makes me feel right. But I wish she wouldn't keep putting me on the spot like this. How can I explain to her how my mother looks at things?

"What you said before," says Yolanda. "All that stuff about shutting you out."

I look at her then.

"You the only one who gets to do the shutting out? That some kind of white privilege?"

"That's not fair."

"No?"

"Okay, I lied, but I did it to keep from hurting your feelings."

"I'll take care of my own feelings. Just don't lie to me."

I meet her look and whisper that I'm sorry.

But she's charged up about this. She wants more than that. She takes the dog's leash away from me, so she'll have all my attention. "Promise me," she says. Her voice is soft, the words like a wish. But she's daring me, challenging me to something that can rarely happen with me.

In so many ways, my whole self is a lie. It's the way I live. I pretend. I'm a name on an assignment paper, the girl in the third seat in the fifth row, but beyond that I don't claim to be anything, because no one would want to know the real me. I pretend I don't need other people. If I let my guard down, I'll get it in the teeth. Like when I got used to the spot next to Ellen Reynolds in math class. She was starting to talk to me. She was pretty much the only person who did. I thought maybe we could be friends. Then Mrs. Kirshin moved our seats; it was time to "move the chess pieces," she said. Marilyn Podswicki got put next to me, and so I smiled at her, but she made such a point of turning away that I froze, right along with the stupid grin on my face. I looked over at Ellen. She was chatting away with her new neighbor, more friendly than she'd ever been with me. I felt like a dirty tissue.

Being honest with people—espcially about wanting them to like me—is a bad idea. It makes me feel like a baby, like I need someone to comfort me or make things turn out differently. But nobody really cares how I feel or how things are for me. And even if they do—'cause sometimes I'm sure my mother does care—there's nothing, absolutely nothing they can do to change things. So I'm better off pretending.

I look at Yolanda. She's waiting for me to answer her. Yolanda makes me feel like I'm really here, the real me, not someone I've put together to get by for the moment. Still, she's seen only bits and pieces of me, and I'm afraid to promise her that I'll never lie, never cover up. I'm not sure

I'd really know how to do that. But I promise anyway, not because I think I can, but because she really wants me to.

Dusty spots them first, practically pulls Yolanda off her feet as she jerks on the leash. Yolanda can't hold her, and the dog runs to David in feverish glee, as if he's been away for days. It's only been about twenty-five minutes. Still, it's been long enough to make him look different. His eyes are red and the sullenness seems to be gone. He kneels and buries his face in the dog's fur in a way that seems to be less about missing the dog than just being glad to have someone to hold on to.

His mom looks awful, too. The sadness is dragging her face down, and her eyes have mascara shadows like my mom's in the morning, and they're even redder than David's. But she smiles at us right away, starts thanking us as if we've saved the dog's life or something. We tell her she's welcome, and Yolanda is already walking away when the woman says, "Wait. Where are you headed?"

Neither of us answers, since we don't exactly know.

"David tells me he knows you. Can I drop you off somewhere? My car is just a block away."

"Sure," Yolanda tells her. "That would be great. Thanks."

I nod and go along with things, wondering where Yolanda is going to tell her to take us. The three of us head down the street, with David and the dog a little bit ahead. I want to ask the woman how her mom is, but I'm afraid to, 'cause it doesn't look as if they got very good news from the doctors.

"I'm Yolanda Baker," Yolanda tells her. "This is Fiona O'Doherty."

"Nice to meet you. I'm Ruth Silverman," she says, and it sounds like she's going to start another round of thank-yous, but instead she asks what brought us to the hospital, wants to know if we were visiting a friend.

"Actually, I was the patient. I have a cracked rib," says Yolanda, sounding proud of it, and for a moment I'm afraid she's going to tell Mrs. Silverman how she got it.

But Yolanda doesn't tell her the truth, and I'm glad. I don't think Mrs. Silverman needs to hear all that. She looks like a nice lady, not the kind who has much to do with little brown bags or people who get their ribs cracked for carrying 'em. Yolanda says something about a collision at a volleyball net, and Mrs. Silverman doesn't seem to give it much thought.

Up ahead, David and Dusty slow down by a Ford station wagon that must be their car. Mrs. Silverman opens the front door, and Dusty leaps in and jumps over the front seat into the back. David reaches around to lift the lock on the back door and climbs in next to the dog. Yolanda and I are not sure where we should go till Mrs. Silverman directs the two of us into the front seat. The inside of the car is warm, nothing a few open windows won't fix. But Mrs. Silverman doesn't open one. Instead she turns the car on and starts fiddling with knobs. Then the sound of rushing air and a funny smell come at us. The car's got air conditioning. I have no trouble reading the look Yolanda shoots me. This lady must be well-off.

"So where are you two headed?" Mrs. Silverman says. I wait to hear what Yolanda will say, 'cause I still don't have any idea. Dusty has her paws over the back of the front seat, panting into our ears. She seems just as interested in the answer as Mrs. Silverman.

"Crotona Park North. 750," Yolanda tells her. That's Mrs. Carson's address. She's a lady Yolanda knows.

"Oh, that's fine. That's not far from us," she says. "We're right on 172nd Street, near Southern Boulevard." She pulls out quickly, now that she knows where she's going. The Dodge she cuts off blares its horn, but she seems completely unaware of it.

"Mom," David scolds from the back.

"What is it, David?"

"You just cut that guy off." He sounds thoroughly embarrassed.

Mrs. Silverman glances in her rearview mirror, as if to figure out what could be wrong. "I certainly didn't mean to," she says. "He looks fine to me." From the backseat comes a groan, but Mrs. Silverman doesn't comment on it. She sits up straighter though, maybe to keep from missing anything else important. "So where do you girls go to school?" she says. She leans forward just a bit to see me better, and I can see she's hoping I'll answer this time. I don't. I hate when normal people ask me questions like this. My family's situation is hardly ever normal, and right now things are even more twisted than usual. Where would I start? *Well, Mrs. Silverman, right now I go to the same school as my cousins, up near Bathgate Avenue, 'cause that's who we've been living with since the eviction. But just a few weeks ago I was going to the school near Mapes Avenue 'cause that's where we moved to when we left my dad in March, but I used to go to school with Yolanda when my family lived on Bryant Avenue, when we were still a family.*

At times like these, it's better to just lie. Which is what I am about to do when Yolanda answers instead, casual as can be.

"Fiona goes to number 11; I go to number 6. But Fiona went to number 6 last year, too. That's how we know David. He was in eighth grade then."

"Of course. So you live on Crotona Park North?"

"We don't live there. A friend of ours lives there."

"Oh, oh, I see. I know that building. I have a friend who lives there." She turns to the back to get confirmation from David. "750. Isn't that Mrs. Carson's building?"

"I think so," David tells her.

"Mrs. Carson is your friend?" says Yolanda.

"Well, an acquaintance really. But we've gotten to be close very quickly. We went to the march together."

"The march?" I say, 'cause I'm wondering if she belongs to SNCC, too, like Yolanda's aunt Cheryl, and goes marching in the South.

"Yes, the march on Washington in August. David came with us."

Yolanda's jaw hasn't exactly dropped, but she's impressed. So am I, actually. When they show footage on TV of the people who went to the march on Washington, you can see that a lot of them were white. I keep wondering where they're from. I never meet any of them around here. I don't know any white person except President Kennedy who has the courage to stand up for colored people's civil rights. Most white people don't want to give them any at all. And now I'm actually meeting one.

"You went to Washington," Yolanda says, turning to David.

"It was really something," he tells her, "except for all the singing on the bus. That drove me nuts."

"Anyway, I'm not sure 750 is Mrs. Carson's building, but I know she lives near the park," says Mrs. Silverman.

"Oh, it is Mrs. Carson's building," says Yolanda. "That's who we're going to see. Mrs. Carson is a good friend of mine." Yolanda crosses her legs in a grown-up kind of way, and I'm wondering why she's getting such a kick out of all this. The whole thing is making me uncomfortable. I liked it better when I thought we were total strangers to Mrs. Silverman. There was no need to tell Mrs. Silverman who we were visiting. Sometimes Yolanda makes me so mad.

"What a small world," says Mrs. Silverman. She's really interested now, and I'm glad we're almost there so this ride can be over. "And how did you meet Mrs. Carson?"

"Mrs. Carson came to talk at our school last year. To the Drama Club. And she knows my aunt Cheryl."

"You're Cheryl Baker's niece? The young woman who does the tutoring?

"Yes!"

"That's a wonderful thing she's doing." Mrs. Silverman is talking about the kids that come to Yolanda's house to get help learning how to read. Some grown-ups come, too, Yolanda says. Their living room is filled with extra chairs so everyone can have a place to sit.

"Yes," Yolanda says, in her grown-up tone. "I help her as much as I can." This is news to me.

"You mean with the tutoring?"

"Yes, I take the little ones sometimes. Aunt Cheryl says it's better to start early, before things get too bad."

"Well, that's important work you're doing. You're going to make a difference in the world." Yolanda doesn't contradict her on that, but at least she doesn't make a big deal out of it. She just sort of smiles.

"Do you help with the tutoring too, Fiona?" says Mrs. Silverman. She's turning to look at me again, but I don't have to answer since David interrupts from the back to yell at her to watch out for the people crossing in front of the car. She slams on the brake.

"Didn't you see them get off the bus?" he scolds her.

"Calm down, David. I didn't hit anyone," she tells him, but she's pretty shaken up. It was a close call. A man in a dark blue work uniform has stopped in the middle of the street to shout at her. Some kids on the corner are laughing. David slides down low in the backseat. "Well, don't they know better than to walk out into traffic?" she says, pleading her case.

"Mrs. Silverman, I think they had the light," Yolanda whispers.

Mrs. Silverman is shocked by this. She puts her hand to her forehead, as if wondering how she could have done such a thing. "I'm so sorry," she says to everyone. I feel bad for her. She has a lot on her mind, her mom dying and all.

"Everything's okay," I tell her. "No one got hurt."

"Mom, go," David calls harshly from the back. "The light is green."

She gives the Ford too much gas and it jerks forward, then smooths itself out, and we're moving along again. Mrs. Silverman grips the steering wheel tightly and looks ahead, but she's upset.

Everybody stays quiet for a while till Yolanda decides to pick up where we left off. "Fiona doesn't do any tutoring yet. I keep telling her she'd be good at it."

Don't ask me where this came from. Yolanda and I have never talked about my doing any tutoring at her aunt's house. But Mrs. Silverman reads some meaning into what Yolanda says, because she answers as if she's trying to help Yolanda convince me to do it. "You should give that serious thought, Fiona. It's a chance to help in the community," she says, but her words have no energy. Her thoughts are elsewhere.

I don't answer her. I laugh to myself at the phrase "help in the community" and the picture it puts in my head: I'm wearing a lily-white crisscross apron, right out of Clara Barton's closet, and I'm walking past Gerrity's Tavern, waving to my dad and his drinking buddies, the ones still upright on their stools, as I head out to assist the community.

Mrs. Silverman is looking at me again. "My mom was a teacher," she says weakly, as if it's something that doesn't matter anymore.

Everybody's quiet for a while, and soon we're on Mrs. Carson's block. Mrs. Silverman slows the car and moves toward the curb, then pulls away again.

"Mom, what are you doing?" says David.

"I'm looking for a parking space."

"Why do we need a parking space? We're just dropping them off."

"I think we should go up and say hello," says Mrs. Silverman. Her voice sounds thin.

"Aw, Mom. Do we have to?" Something about David's voice makes the dog give out a whine of her own.

"No, we don't have to, but I'd like to," she says and slows the car again. This time it's really a parking spot and not a fire hydrant. "And anyway, it feels like we ought to. After all, what an odd coincidence that Fiona and Yolanda should be coming here of all places. It's like fate."

Yolanda and I exchange a look. "I can walk home from

here," David tells her. He and the dog are sitting forward now, eager to get out.

Mrs. Silverman stops in the middle of trying to park, her concentration broken, and gives David a look. When he doesn't say anything, she says, "You could at least come up and say hello." David rolls his eyes. He thinks he's earned more than enough points in visiting his grandmother. He lets himself out of the car before his mother finishes getting into the spot, but he doesn't walk away. He waits with the dog, staring down the street like a soldier held against his will.

4

Mrs. Carson's apartment looks just as neat and feminine as it did the first time I was here, two weeks ago, the day after I ran away and spent the night on a park bench. The skeleton is still taped to the outside of her door, and we duck through the spiders that bob from strings tied to the ceiling of her hallway. But Mrs. Carson looks different. Her eyes are bare and pale—without her false eyelashes—and not welcoming. She's tied her curly hair back tightly with a rubber band, something my mother says you should never use because it can damage your hair. I want to tell Mrs. Carson this. I kind of like her hair, even though the dark roots are showing today. Her voice sounds different, too, but I can still hear Dinah Shore in it. She tells us how surprised she is and how delighted to see us, but it's not like before. Something's wrong. I look at Yolanda to see if she's noticed it, too. She has.

"I'm afraid you've caught me in the middle of my chores," Mrs. Carson says as she moves us into the living room. She lifts a laundry basket off the couch and takes some folded clothes off the coffee table. She disappears with them into the bedroom, along with the blouses she's hung from the back of a wing chair. Dusty gets away from David and accompanies her on these trips as if the rooms beyond are dangerous and require her watch.

"Oh, Louise, please don't fuss," Mrs. Silverman tells her. "We were just dropping the girls off and I thought I'd come up and say hello, see how you're doing."

"Please sit down," Mrs. Carson says, looking confused. "Yolanda, I thought you were still in the hosp—"

"Oh, I'm fine," Yolanda says, but anybody can see by the careful way she lowers herself onto the chair that she's not. "It's a long story."

Mrs. Carson doesn't ask her to explain, but she looks doubtful. She turns to Mrs. Silverman to tell her that she didn't know we all knew each other.

"We didn't," Mrs. Silverman says, taking a seat at one end of a Victorian couch. "Well, David did. But I just met the girls today when I arrived at the hospital. I rushed there when the doctor called, and they were in the lobby, and I asked them to mind Dusty for us. They were so helpful."

Mrs. Carson looks puzzled. "But why did you bring Dusty with you to the hospital?"

"Well, she hasn't been behaving very well around the house. I mean ever since my mom went into the hospital, she keeps roaming the rooms for her, and when we leave her alone in the place, we come back to some unpleasant surprises."

"It wasn't her fault," David says. "You forgot to walk her that morning. It was your turn."

"She's not herself," Mrs. Silverman insists.

"Well, it's a difficult time for all of you," says Mrs. Carson. "How is she, Ruth?"

Mrs. Silverman doesn't answer. She shakes her head and begins to pull on her collar and then on her ear, as if searching for some button that will keep her from starting to cry. But she doesn't find one, and the next thing we know she's covering her mouth with her hand and bowing her head, and the tears are in full gear.

David shifts his weight, wanting to be anywhere but here. Mrs. Carson sits close to Mrs. Silverman on the couch. "I'm so sorry," Mrs. Carson says, putting her arm around her.

David announces that Dusty needs to go out. This is news to the dog, who has settled herself into the folded towels that fell off the arm of a chair. But she gets up when she hears her name and moves close to David, ready to follow. David's mother doesn't say anything, but Mrs. Carson nods at David as if he's chosen just the right thing to do.

"We'll go with you," says Yolanda, and in a few steps we're out the door.

Dragging her leash behind her down the stairs, Dusty reaches the lobby first. We watch her pace back and forth in front of the glass doors, her tail keeping time with a panting tongue. She glances back at David as if to tell him how important it is to get outside.

"Well," I say, "she seems to know what she wants."

"Not like a lot of people I know." David picks up the leash as Yolanda opens the door.

"Who are you talking about? Your mom?" says Yolanda.

"It's nothing. Forget it."

He doesn't need to say so. I can see how easily he loses patience with his mother. I know what he means about her. She does get flustered easily, like each moment is an emergency she hadn't planned for. She's so different from my mother. Maybe that's because if my mother allows any doubts in, any other way of doing things, the chaos will take over and she'll lose her way completely. Still, I don't really understand why David finds his mother so annoying. I see how confused she gets and how frightened of everything she seems to be, but she treats him like a prince. *Please, David* this, and *Would you mind, David?* that. She's so polite and gentle with him. How can you fault somebody like that? The only time my mother says please is to a grown-up, somebody she thinks really matters.

The dog leads us east along the park. She sniffs suspiciously here and there as if every tree and fire hydrant is something she can't trust until she checks it out herself. The three of us are doing about the same thing to each other. We steal glances, consider a question or something to say, then think better of it. "I remember you two from school last year," David tells us finally, as if landing on something safe. "You're in eighth grade now, right?"

"Yes," says Yolanda. "I remember you." I cross my fingers,

hoping that Yolanda won't start telling everything about us. But David doesn't exactly ask. He just starts talking about how different high school is. He's a freshman at James Monroe High School, near 172nd Street.

I ask him if he knows Liam—he's a senior—and he nods like he'd rather avoid the subject. Liam isn't a member of the Celts, the Irish gang from the top of the park, but he's close with some of the guys who are.

Nobody says much for a long while. We get to Southern Boulevard and turn right. Dusty seems to know where she wants to go, so we just follow along. "Can I ask you something?" I say.

"Guess so," says David, but he doesn't promise an answer.

"How come you get so mad at your mom?"

"I'm not mad really."

"You don't have much patience with her. And her mom is so sick and all. It's gotta be a rough time."

"She's always having a rough time." Everybody's quiet for about a block, but David picks it up again once we're out of range of the people waiting on line for the bus. The words break out of him like steam. "There isn't a single day when there isn't some kind of tragedy going on with her. If she forgets to fill an ice cube tray, she's convinced she's a bad mother."

"My mom gets like that," I say, but she's more likely to blame one of us. If Liam forgets to take out the garbage, she tells him he'll infest the building with rats.

"You don't understand. If I get a bad grade, it's not about me; it's about how *she* failed. And if Dad's in a bad mood, she can't just pour him a glass of wine or tell him a joke; she's got to probe to find out what's at the heart of it—but all she really wants to figure out is what *she's* done wrong. And if there's nothing going wrong that day, she'll latch onto something from the day before or something from the newspaper. She thinks the Berlin Wall is her own personal crisis just because her second cousin still lives over there."

"Yup," says Yolanda. "Grown-ups get real confused about why they're doing things. They like to say it's for us. But mostly it's about what they want. That's if you can even believe the reasons they give you."

We get to the corner of 173rd Street and have to wait for the light. "And when is it safe to believe what *you two* are saying?" David says. The words are harsh, but his tone is good-natured.

The question is for me, but I just give him a blank look.

"Mrs. Carson wasn't expecting you. Where were you really supposed to be going when you left the hospital?"

"What do you mean?" I ask. I don't know what else to say.

"I mean there's something phony with you," he says. "Maybe you're fooling my mom, but I could tell from the start that you're in some kind of trouble."

"We're not in trouble," I say.

"Not yet, anyway," says Yolanda, and I want to kick her.

"So where were you really headed?"

"We don't know yet," she says, and this time I groan out loud.

"What's that mean?" he says.

"I wasn't exactly released from the hospital today."

"Then how did you get out?"

"Mostly walked."

David doesn't see the light change 'cause he's too busy laughing. "Wait a minute," he says, looking first at me, then at Yolanda, wondering, I bet, if either of us is telling the truth yet. "What about your folks? Isn't this going to be a slight problem?"

"They're the problem," Yolanda says. David doesn't say anything. We cross the street. But I just want to walk the other way, go off by myself, and let Yolanda say whatever she wants as long as it's not about me.

Dusty heads down 172nd Street and starts pulling hard on the leash. David has the strap wrapped around his wrist, and he has to grip it hard.

"What's she all excited about?" I ask him.

"This is where we live," David says.

"Oh," I say. It's one of those six-family houses and looks as if it's well taken care of. The wrought-iron railing isn't spotted with rust, and some yellow mums are planted in the little patch of ground between the railing and the building.

"Why don't you come up? I've got to feed her."

I look at Yolanda, and she answers for us. "Sure," she says, and I nod so she'll see it's okay with me.

5

Dusty flies down the hall and makes straight for what's clearly her signature spot on the couch in the living room. Yolanda and I watch her go, not sure what to do, till David says, "Go ahead. Just follow the hound."

We pass a kitchen and some other rooms off the long hall that leads to the living room. Dusty is sprawled on the white, curving sofa, her tail wagging leisurely, as if waving us in to join her. But we don't sit down. Yolanda begins peeking at the photographs here and there while I wander to some shelves in the corner where a collection of glass figurines catches the light from the double windows. One piece is a carousel and the horses have little hints of color near their saddles. I'm dying to pick up one of the figurines, but I don't dare. The angel figures are even more tempting, so I decide I'd better step away.

A long stereo cabinet lines the wall, and someone's left some album covers on top. They're old, with edges all soft and gray, and mostly from Broadway shows. They don't interest me, but I pick one up to read the liner notes and feel Yolanda next to me. She's whispering about what a nice place they have.

"Sure is," I tell her. "Nicest apartment I've ever been in." We hear a sound from the kitchen, like cabinets closing, and Dusty is off the couch like a shot, heading for the kitchen. David doesn't come out right away, and we start to wonder what he's up to. We hear him talking to the dog, then nothing for a minute or two, till he calls out to us to put a record on. Yolanda picks an album by some guy named John Coltrane. "The rest is mostly old-fogy stuff," she whispers. She lowers the phonograph needle onto the record and the room fills up real slow with the sound of a saxophone.

When David comes out, he's carrying a bottle of something and three glasses. The glasses have a gray tinge and long stems, and they sparkle in the light as he moves toward us. He puts them down on the coffee table and asks if we'd like some wine, like it's no big deal.

There's no need to answer because he's already pouring. I watch the stuff gurgle out of the long neck and into the pretty glasses. It reminds me of a scene from a movie. I sneak a look at Yolanda, but she doesn't look the least bit nervous about all this. I think maybe she's just a way better faker than I am. I look over my shoulder toward the hall that leads to the apartment door. "David, what if your mom comes home?" I say. He looks at me funny, and I wish I hadn't said it. He's going to think I'm a little grammar school kid for sure, but I can't help it. This is nuts. "I mean, wouldn't she get pissed at you for this?"

"Yup," he says, "she'd go crazy."

"Maybe we better not, then," says Yolanda.

"Don't worry about it. When she and Mrs. Carson start talking, they can't stop. She won't be back here for hours." He sits down on the couch, motioning for us to join him.

Yolanda and I don't say anything, and he can see we're not convinced. "Since my grandmother got sick, it's worse. The last time she went to Mrs. Carson's, she wound up staying overnight."

We sit down, although I'm not convinced the white sofa is meant for anyone to use. Yolanda still doesn't say anything or reach for the glass. Neither do I.

"Relax," David laughs. "Have some."

The thing is, I don't really want any. David lifts his glass like he's at a cocktail party in some Cary Grant movie. Yolanda follows his lead. But I don't get how you're supposed to drink fancy wine in a fancy glass. My dad drinks only beer and doesn't usually bother with a glass. I can't remember ever having wine in our house. Grandma says it's a Protestant drink. My brother says it's for fairies. David sniffs the rim of the glass, then takes a sip, a large one, and so does Yolanda. I watch for her reaction. Her nose twitches and her mouth puckers.

Finally, she looks at me. "Well?" she says.

I put the glass to my mouth and let my lips get wet, but I don't actually take a sip. Still, I can sort of taste it, and I don't like it much.

"I guess you guys don't drink wine very often," David says.

"Not very often," Yolanda tells him.

Something tells me it's a lot less than that, but in my case it's more like never, so I don't contradict her. Drinking in my family is not for amateurs. They don't care what kind of glass it's in or what it smells like. They drink to get drunk, and when they get there, all hell can break loose. But maybe wine can't do that to you, because David and Yolanda don't look too worried about it.

David moves some pillows into place behind him on the couch and settles back with his feet up on the coffee table. His legs are long and his thighs look solid under his jeans. He doesn't have his jacket on anymore, and you can see there's hair on his forearms. He doesn't look like a fairy to me. I hear a kind of sigh from him, then he takes another sip of the wine.

"Your apartment is really beautiful," I say. "Really nice."

"Thank you," he says, and he looks at me a long time as if there's something about me he can't figure out. "Where do you live again?"

Yolanda comes to my rescue with a question about the march on Washington. "Tell us about the march," she insists. "What made your mother want to go?"

"I'm not sure what it's about for my mom. She says it's about civil rights and all that, but I think she feels guilty for having a mostly easy life."

"You mean having money?" says Yolanda.

David nods. "She wants to make sure I see how many people don't have it so easy."

"So what's wrong with that?" Yolanda says.

"Nothing. But I shouldn't have to feel bad about not being poor. If some people have it rough, that's not my fault."

"Whose fault is it?" Yolanda asks him, and I think of my mom trying to get a place of her own, away from a man who thinks he's got the right to use her and her sons as punching bags. Is it her fault when she can't keep up with the rent?

"I don't know," he says, frustrated. "I see it as two separate things."

"So does everybody else," says Yolanda. "That's why it's like we got two separate countries. Black and white."

"Yes, but—"

"So tell us about the march," I say, interrupting David's answer, 'cause I don't want to hear any more about whose fault it is when you're poor. I brace myself and taste the wine. It's fruity and sweet, really not that bad.

David sits back. "Intense," he says. "So many people. Everybody being so nice to each other. Talking. Sharing food. Like we were on some other planet."

"My aunt Cheryl was there. She works with SNCC," Yolanda explains to David.

David nods. "My mom goes to CORE meetings." David reads the question on my face. "Congress of Racial Equality," he says.

Jeez, a whole other world is going on out there, and my family doesn't know anything about it.

"Fiona, you know who they are," Yolanda insists. "They

were the Freedom Riders, two years ago. Remember? It was in all the papers."

And then I do, because the pictures were on the front page. "You mean the people who went down South to protest segregation on the buses?"

"Yup. Two years ago. 1961."

My mother insisted they were communist infiltrators, but I remember thinking they were so brave. The white protesters sat in the back of the buses and the colored protesters sat in the front, and then when they got to the bus stations, the colored protesters went into the whites-only sections. And, man, there was hell to pay, 'cause the white mobs in Alabama and Mississippi were so mad they attacked the riders. They even firebombed a bus. That was the first I heard about it really, because the *Daily News* ran a picture of the bus on fire.

"My dad says he doesn't have time for stuff like that," David says. "Fighting for a cause is for people who don't have to make a living."

"That's not true," Yolanda says. "The people who went to Washington are just ordinary folks."

"I know," he says, getting annoyed. "I was there. Anyway, my dad was busy *making a living* that day." He drags the words out, lets his feelings show this time. "So I got roped into minding my mom."

"Minding your mom?" I say.

"You saw what she's like."

"She does seem a little lost sometimes," says Yolanda.

"That's my mom," says David.

My mom is nothing like Mrs. Silverman. My mom says you can count on things going wrong. It's the good things she gets suspicious about, wondering how life might be setting her up.

We drink more of the wine. It's making a feeling in the top of my head that's very strange. It's like there might be an opening there. My head doesn't feel nearly as heavy to hold up. The strange thing is I never thought of my head as heavy before now. Anyway, I touch the top of my head every now and then to see if everything's all right.

"Do you know the freckles on your arm are arranged like a baseball field?" David says to me.

"What?" I say, ready to laugh.

"Look," he says, touching each freckle in turn, "here's home plate, here's first base, second, third. You've even got a shortstop."

I grin, but I can't answer him. His touch on my forearm tickles. And anyway, I don't think a boy has ever touched me before. You can't really count Artie Cushman holding my hands when we have to square dance in gym. Anyway, Artie touches you like he's got hold of a fish out of a basket and wants to drop it back in.

"Dusty," David says, calling the dog to him. She obeys happily.

"You're a good dog, aren't you, Dusty?" Yolanda says.

Dusty wags her tail, delighted with the attention. She gives out a sudden bark as if in agreement, and when we laugh at this, she gets even more excited and jumps up into the tiny space between me and Yolanda, the way fat people claim subway seats three sizes too small for them and expect the world to adjust.

"Sorry about that," says David. "She likes the attention."

"Yup," says Yolanda, "everybody likes attention." And I'm pretty sure she's looking at me as if she's annoyed, except I can't be sure, 'cause I'm too busy touching the top of my head to find out where that swooshing sound is coming from. It's a soft, breathing sound that repeats and repeats, and I think maybe it's the brain gases escaping from the new hole in the top of my head.

But before I can find out what Yolanda is upset about, David stands up and says, "I'll get it," as if we all know what he means, but I don't. David crosses the room to the record player and it dawns on me that the record is over. That swooshing is the sound the needle makes when it reaches the end. I laugh so hard I have to put my glass down.

David puts on Bob Dylan and comes back to the couch. "Are you okay?" he says.

"I'm fine," I tell him. I go to pick up the glass of wine again, but David moves it out of my reach.

"Better not," he says. "Guess people don't do much drinking in your family." I don't answer. It would be nice to let him think that.

"What's on your other arm? Goalposts?" David says, reaching across to inspect. I laugh, but he takes my arm, my right arm this time, and pretends he suspects something else altogether. "You're an agent, aren't you," he whispers at me.

"What?" I say. I think I've heard him right, but "A Hard Rain's Gonna Fall" is going full blast now, so I can't be sure.

"You're an agent."

"What are you talking about?"

"You can tell me. It's okay."

"Tell you what?"

He leans closer, begins to connect some freckles with his fingers. Finally, he stops at one that's larger than any close to it. "See that formation?" I look, try to recognize a football field or something, but can't. "That's the exact configuration of the missile bases photographed over Cuba last year." I look at my arm again, and this makes him grin, but he keeps at it. "Ingenious. Who would ever think to search the forearms of eighth-graders in the Bronx for a cache of Cold War information. What's *she* got on her arm? U-2 flight patterns over Russia?"

Yolanda rolls her eyes. I guess she thinks David is pretty corny. "What's with you?" Yolanda says, but David holds out his hand and demands to see her arm.

"He thinks we're spies," I tell her. "He wants to see if you have freckles, too."

But Yolanda's not ready to drop her "I'm too cool for this" attitude.

David shrugs it off. "I'll go get us some pretzels," he says, and heads for the kitchen.

Bob Dylan is singing, "'How many roads must a man

walk down before they call him a man?'" and he sounds
old to me, although I know he isn't. It isn't his voice really,
but the tone, the attitude in it, like he knows there's barely
any point in asking the question. Peter, Paul & Mary sing
"Blowin' in the Wind" like they're angry, like they're fed up
with how long some things have to go on before somebody
changes something. But Dylan sings like he knows that
things can stay really bad pretty much forever. "You like this
song?" I ask Yolanda.

"I do," she says.

"I bet your aunt Cheryl likes it."

"She's got his first album."

"Does she ever get discouraged sometimes?"

"She doesn't like to talk like that."

"I know, but things don't always change. They don't
always have a happy ending."

"Still, you can't just give up," she says.

"When Peter, Paul & Mary sing this, it sounds like it's
about big ideas and great causes. Dylan sings it like it could
be about one person's story. Like mine, even."

"What do you mean?"

"I mean, how long can you wait for things to change?
For my father to stop drinking? How many times do we
have to watch him beat up my mom before we do something
about it? Where's the answer to that one?"

Yolanda nods, like she knows exactly what I mean.

"And what about you? How long will it be before you
get back once your mother takes you to South Carolina?"

"Won't be long at all 'cause I'm not going to South Carolina."

"But how are you going to get out of it? How long do you think you can stay away from home today before they come after you? You can't keep this up forever."

"I know that," Yolanda says, a little angry. "I'm going home. I just wasn't ready to see her yet. That's all."

"But leaving the hospital is only going to make her angry. It will make it worse."

"Could make them see I'm serious about this."

"Serious? What are you going to do, walk to school from South Carolina?" I sound panicky, as if I'm going to lose her for sure.

"I said I'm not going, Fiona. And I'm not."

"I hope not," I say, and I feel myself starting to cry. "I don't know what's going to happen to me if you're gone."

"Fiona, everything will be okay. I'm not going anywhere. But I swear, sometimes you talk as if you don't have a self of your own, like you're some piece of newspaper in the street, flying any way the wind blows."

Now I'm crying hard.

"You've got to make up your mind who you are," she says.

I don't understand what she means. What choice do I have about who I am? I'm stuck in a family of maniacs. I can't change anything. I look at her face, thinking maybe I've misunderstood the question. I touch the top of my head again, because the weight of my head still feels so strange, so light. "What are you talking about?" I say.

"If you don't decide who you are, people are going to be bossing you around all the time." I shrug. This is silly. Can't she see who I am? Everybody in my life but Owen gets to boss me around.

"So tell me one thing about who you are that nobody but you gets to decide."

I don't answer her.

"Don't you even have something you *want* to be?"

This time I understand the question. It covers a lot of territory, 'cause I want to be just about everybody I see. Anybody but me would do, really. But I know Yolanda's not going to want to hear that. She's looking at me as if all I have to do is step into this, as if surely I've thought about this and made some decisions about what my future will be. It's giving me a headache. "Yolanda ..."

"God, Fiona. There's got to be something you want to be."

"Yeah," I say. "Sure. There's something." I look at her, wondering whether I should say this, whether she'll even know what I'm talking about. "I want to be normal, just normal," I answer, and the word feels like something forbidden to say, like a curse. "I want to be in a family that has its own place to live. I want to go to school and talk about what other kids talk about—what they had for dinner, the shows they watched on TV." Yolanda puts her finger to her lips to quiet me. My voice is getting loud, and she knows I wouldn't want David to hear this. "I want a father who doesn't scare the hell out of us," I whisper.

Something comes over Yolanda's face then. I watch it change her eyes. For a second, I'm afraid that I've upset her. But then I see she's just off track, doesn't know what to say. She puts her hand on mine to comfort me. Her skin is so dark, so different, and it reminds me that even this, my friendship with Yolanda, is not normal, not the way things are supposed to be.

"You know what your problem is?" Yolanda says. I look at her, puzzled. "You believe everything you see." I still don't get it. She leans in close to whisper in my ear. "All those 'normal' people you think you see out there? They're crazy as bedbugs."

I laugh and Yolanda starts laughing, too, so I don't hear the key turn in the lock, only Dusty barking. And I don't hear the footsteps, only the sound of my father calling my name as he stands in the entrance to the living room with Mrs. Silverman and Yolanda's aunt Cheryl.

Even before I open my eyes, I know I'm in a different place. I smell no diapers, none of my aunt's stifling room fresheners. It must be morning. But barely. There's no traffic yet, no coffeepot burping, only the smell of stale cigarette smoke, that ghostly trail that hangs back after my father leaves a room. I move my hand slowly out from my side, and as soon as I make contact with the wall, I know where I am—my dad's place, on Bryant Avenue, in my old room.

I open my eyes and get up onto my elbows. I turn to look out the window, but before anything can register I have to lower myself back down—as gently as I possibly can—because I have a headache like no other headache I've ever had. How did I get here? I try to put things in reverse, retrace my steps. But I can't think. My head is screaming at me, and my tongue feels like it's tripled its size. Somebody must have made me suck sandpaper last night. A flash of being with Yolanda breaks through, like a whiff of something clean, and I remember having such a good time with her and David. And then I remember the rest—my father standing there with Cheryl and Mrs. Silverman, both looking not so happy at all. I reach down to touch my shin because it's hurting, as if on cue, and I remember walking into a table or something as I left the place. Oh, God. What a jerk I looked like in front of everyone. It all comes back in a flood now. Mrs. Silverman scolding David. Yolanda giving Cheryl a hard time. My father taking me down to the car. My head was spinning, like when you get off the Tilt-a-Whirl at Coney Island, only it wouldn't go away. But what happened to Yolanda? Cheryl must have taken her home; her mother was probably waiting there. I look at the window again; it's barely light. Her mother couldn't have taken her away yet, could she? Maybe I can get there in time. Before they leave. I could see her before she leaves, say good-bye, get her address or something.

I look around the room; it's odd the things I left here, the things I didn't take with me when we left to be on our own. I didn't want us to be with my father anymore, but I didn't want to move again either. I remember thinking that if I left enough things here—my old dolls, some clothes—that we'd have to come back. Maybe *he* would move away instead. And I could be back in my regular school with Yolanda

It's funny the things you treasure about a place. On the wall at the head of my bed within arm's reach is a small shelf, only about a foot long. I used to keep a candle on it—which my mother never wanted me to light—and what-ever book I was reading. I loved that shelf and the way the candle looked on it. The shelf has a brace underneath each side and each one is carved into curves and tiny recesses, and in the place where each brace meets the shelf there's a rose, a wooden rose. The edge of the shelf is a smooth, curvy line that I used to trace with my finger. The thing looks like it came from some really fine home. It would have been just an afterthought in a room full of elegant furniture. This shelf definitely doesn't belong here. It has an attitude. You can't put just anything on it. It has to be something with character. It can keep a secret, too. The brace closer to the window—the side you can't see—has a little space behind it. It isn't flush against the wall. The space is just enough to slide a folded paper into. That's where I'd hide whatever poem I was writing.

I reach up to see if anything is there. There is. I pull it out. It's a piece of notebook paper with just a few lines on it, umbrellas and daisies doodled in the margins. What junk. Corny junk. You'd never find Yolanda wasting her time on poetry.

The light coming in makes the room look even more unfamiliar, maybe because I'm never up this early. I pull myself up to peek out the window. The sunlight is playing on the glass of the building across the alley, but it's being pretty shy about it. Maybe even the sun isn't so sure today about how things are supposed to go. Nothing is moving. A cat is sitting down there between a couple of garbage cans, but he's not moving at all. He's got a look on his face that makes it clear he's totally disgusted with what's become of the neighborhood. The weak light outside and the lightness in my head make things feel like they're suspended, as if Yolanda is tucked away somewhere waiting, as if whatever my mother knows or doesn't know doesn't matter yet. There's only this window, this almost-dark room, this intermission. Still, I close my eyes again, dreading the day, feeling surely I've lost Yolanda now, that there'll be nowhere to go to get away from my family, from the way we surrender to the idea that nothing can really change, the way we settle for gratitude, relief that things aren't worse.

For some reason, that does it. I swing my legs off the side of the bed and drag myself up. I'm still in my clothes, but I can't find my shoes. I don't want to put on a light. I want to get out of here without my father knowing. The bathroom is on the far side of the kitchen, a good distance from my father's room, but I get my business done as quietly as I can. The girl in the mirror is like someone who's been caught at something. I didn't know I looked that guilty. But I comb my hair, pull it back, and I'm expressionless again, a poster child for nobodies.

Out in the kitchen, there's still no sign of my shoes. So I'm in the living room, hoping I can spot them without putting the light on, when I practically trip over my dad's legs stretched out in front of him. He leaps up like a shot and says my name as if he's been waiting for me to answer a question, like he must have been dreaming about me.

"It's okay, Dad," I say, because he looks so startled.

"Fiona," he says, sitting up, then again, "Oh, Fiona," but

this time it's as if I'm a dreadful reminder of something he was hoping to forget about. I don't bother confirming it's me. "We've got some talking to do, young lady." He rubs the sleep from his face, as if readying himself best he can for the job. "I'm making some coffee," he says, and stands up. He takes my arm. "Come with me." He knows better than to trust that I won't try to run off again once he's out of sight.

He puts the ceiling light on in the kitchen, and I'm amazed at how tidy everything looks. The linoleum is gleaming. The table is clear. The drainer has a few sparkling turned-down glasses, and the sink would pass muster in a doctor's office. "Sit down," he tells me, and gets what he needs for the coffee. I go for my old place at the table, back to the wall, next to where Owen would sit. "Do you want some juice?" he says. "Or are you a coffee drinker now, too?" There's a little scolding in his tone, but mostly sarcasm. I don't answer. "A fine mess you've gotten yourself into. Runnin' off again," he says. He's talking about the first time I ran away, the day we were evicted. He and Liam drove all over looking for me.

"I didn't run off."

"Well, what do you call it, then? Nobody knew where you were."

"She knows where I go."

"Your mother knows you've been goin' to that hospital after school?"

"She just doesn't want to know."

"And what is that supposed to mean?"

"It's been that way ever since the first time I went. She forbid me to go, and I went anyway. She doesn't know what to do about it."

"But you weren't *at* the hospital yesterday. Neither was Yolanda. Her aunt was beside herself when she got there."

"Cheryl called Mom?"

"She couldn't reach your mother. She didn't have Aunt Maggie's number. She came here. And we went lookin' for you."

"So Mom doesn't know? I mean about David's?"

"She knows now. And she's not happy about it, I can tell you that."

"That's nothing new," I mutter, but he hears me.

"This is different. She's worried about you. We both are."

"Worried?" I'm baffled. "Why?"

"Well, you've never been any trouble. She's thrown, is all."

"Thrown?" It sounds almost as if they've been talking about me, considering what to do. It's hard to imagine. I've always figured I was along for the ride, not someone they made decisions about.

"How long have you been doing this?"

I figure he must be talking about the hospital again, so I tell him how I went to visit Yolanda the very next day after she got hurt and that I've been visiting her there nearly every day for two weeks.

"No, I mean the drinking. It's no good, Fiona." I don't

say anything. "I know what I'm talking about." Can't argue with that. "How long has it been going on? Answer me."

"It hasn't," I say. He thinks I've been drinking before. "I mean I've never done that before. It just happened. We didn't plan it." He gives me a suspicious look. "Honest," I say.

But I don't think he believes me. He pours more coffee. "It's got to stop. Do you understand? That's the end of it."

"Dad, it's not what you think. David just thought we'd like some wine."

"David's Jewish, am I right?"

Here we go again, another warning about the ethnic terrors of those "other" people and the need to stay with your own kind. I can't believe my family hasn't figured out by now that diluting the Irish can only improve matters. "What's that got to do with anything?"

"What it's got to do with is genes. Jewish people can take it or leave it. They drink one day; they don't drink the next. It's not an issue. You're made of something else altogether."

I don't know where my dad gets these ridiculous theories from, but he's convinced.

"How do you know that?" I ask.

"The Irish drink like it's their patriotic duty is what I'm sayin'. And every generation of this family has loyalists aplenty." I don't know when my father got so concerned about this pattern. He's pretty strict to the code himself. He sees how I'm looking at him. "I'm off the stuff," he says. "I told you that."

He did. But I don't exactly believe him. Not that I think

he's lying. It's just that I know it won't last. But today is October 29 so it's been eighteen days. I guess that's something. "Tell me," he says, looking worried. "How did the wine make you feel?"

"Fine," I tell him. "It was no big deal." The truth is I felt really good. I felt happy. But it was more than that, 'cause mostly I go around feeling like I've done something wrong. I don't even know what it is. And mostly I haven't even done anything, but I feel bad anyway. But with the wine that feeling was completely gone. I felt just fine, talking and laughing and enjoying the music and just being there with Yolanda and David, not worrying or feeling out of place. And I was able to talk just like anybody else, instead of being tongue-tied.

"And what now? How do you feel this morning?"

"Bad," I whisper.

"Well, don't forget that, because it'll take more drink to feel good the next time. Then more and more until you feel nothin' at all. Nothin'." He raises his voice like he's angry. But he's not angry at me. He's angry at himself. He looks away from me and gets out a cigarette, sinks into himself like he does when he's worrying. Times like this I wonder how he really feels about himself. I remember the first time he had to go to my teacher's conference. Mom had always gone to the conferences every semester, but when she started working, he had to go instead. The first time, it was awful. He was sober as a judge, but when Mrs. Truman asked him a question, he couldn't speak. It was just a normal question, something about math homework, but he was so nervous he couldn't get an answer out. I felt bad for him. When the next conference came along, he had no trouble talking at all. He'd had a few drinks, just enough to loosen him up. That's what he's afraid of, that I'll wind up like him, needing to drink before I can do normal things. But that's never going to happen 'cause I'm nothing like my father, and I never will be.

He doesn't say anything for a long while, and I start wondering how I'm going to tell him that I don't want to go to school. I want to go to Yolanda's house. Dad looks at me. "I want you to give me your word," he says. I dread this. I don't know what he's going to ask, but I can think of a whole slew of promises I don't want to make. "I want your word that there'll be no more drinking."

I breathe out, relieved. "Forget it," I say.

"Forget it, my ass," he says, on his feet now. This, of course, is Dad's more customary way of negotiating, but he's misunderstood me.

"No, Dad. I mean don't worry. I'm not going to drink. You can forget about it. That's all I meant."

He puts his hand through his hair, as if I've given him quite enough grief already. "You can see what it's led to for this family."

And whose fault is that? I want to say, but I don't, because my dad is into another of his phases where he's so sorry and so determined to make things right. Every few months or so, he looks up from the mess he's made of his life and ours and vows never to take a drink again. Times like these, his flagellation would put a monk to shame. He's so penitent he's ready to make amends to the cat for putting her out at night. It doesn't usually last more than a few weeks, but it's long enough to see what he'd be like if he was normal, if he could really stop drinking for good. He plays stickball with Liam and his friends. He reads me his favorite poems. He gives his paycheck to Mom instead of the bartender.

This pledge won't last either, but maybe today I can at least get something out of it. Maybe I can convince him to let me go to Yolanda's. "Dad, I can't go to school today."

"Of course you're goin' to school today. You're going to school and we're getting things straightened out around here."

I don't know what he intends to straighten out, but he needs to understand what's going on with Yolanda. "Dad, you don't understand. Yolanda's mother is here. She came up from South Carolina, and when she goes back, she's taking Yolanda with her."

He looks at me, puzzled. "I don't see what we can do about that."

The truth of what he says makes me even more upset. "I know," I say, "but I want to see her. They might leave today."

"Is that what they're planning?"

"I don't know. Yolanda doesn't know."

"And she probably doesn't even know for sure that her mother's going to take her there. You two just have yourselves all in a dither."

"But she will. She wants Yolanda to be with her."

"Well, a family should be together. That's the key," he says, as if I've hit on the answer to something we've been troubling over.

"But if they leave, I may not see her again."

"Well, call her. See what's going on."

That would be such a relief, although I dread going down to ask Mrs. Olsen if I can use her phone.

"If she's really leaving, I'll take you to say good-bye. But we've got problems of our own to take care of. And we're going to start with getting this family back together."

I look at him, wondering if he realizes what he's saying. Mom will never go back to him. She told us she wouldn't. And Liam says Dad will wind up killing her if she does. There's just no way. Dad's delusional. "I don't know, Dad. I don't think Mom's going to go for that."

"She's got to. We've got no choice. We've got to think about you kids, what all this is doing to you." Dad's never been real good at that before. I don't see how he's going to convince my mother that anything has changed. I don't tell him that 'cause he knows it already.

"I haven't had a drink since the day you ran out of here. Things are going to be different."

Different sure sounds good right now. I can't help thinking about how much better it would be, at least for me. We wouldn't have to live with Aunt Maggie. I'd be in the same school as Yolanda again. Maybe things could change. Maybe Dad really could stop drinking. He's fine when he's not drinking. Everybody knows that. It's got to be worth a try. I look around the room. I imagine us together again, finishing dinner, watching *The Ed Sullivan Show*, maybe getting another dog. But just when it starts to feel good, other images come, and I push them away: The arguing. The way he is when he's coming at her, like a sure winner nobody wants to bet on. Her face when she knows she can't get away. What she looks like when she falls, when a grown woman falls, like something you're not supposed to see. It's not all graceful and feminine, like in the movies. It's ugly and scary, especially when she doesn't get up, but stays there on the floor. And you don't know, not for a long while sometimes, whether she's badly hurt or just feels safer there.

"I'll call Yolanda," I say, and head toward the door.

"It's okay," he says, motioning toward the wall where the phone is. "I paid the phone bill."

Paid the phone bill. Jeez. He probably borrowed money again from Guido Marino on Bathgate Avenue. That's a risky thing to do. Maybe he really will stay sober this time.

Cheryl answers. She's surprised it's me but not annoyed. She asks how I am but hesitantly, as if she's trying not to embarrass me.

"I'm fine." I tell her. "I'm at my dad's. I could come over. I mean if Yolanda is leaving today or something."

"Leaving today?"

"For South Carolina."

The line is quiet for a few seconds, then Cheryl's

voice comes back again, a different tone. Much different. "Yolanda's not going anywhere."

I can't help but believe her. She's so firm about it. Still, it would be good to hear it from Yolanda. "Can I talk to her?" I say.

"She's still sleeping. We were all up late. I'm going to wake her for school soon. Do you want me to have her call you? Where will you be?"

The idea of her going to school today suddenly makes everything much better. She must be staying in New York for sure. "No, that's okay," I say. "Just tell her I called, but I'll catch up with her after school."

"Okay, Fiona. I will."

My father is in my room when I hang up. "Have you got something here you can wear to school?" he says. The question catches me off guard. It's been a long while since he's paid attention to stuff like that. It's a nice feeling.

"Yes, definitely."

"Or we can stop by Aunt Maggie's." I'd rather wear my father's clothes than stop at Aunt Maggie's, and he can see that clearly on my face. "Well, you'd better get yourself ready."

He's right. The sun is full up now, and I move quickly to find some clothes. "Are you going to be talking to Mom today?"

"Yes," he says with a funny look on his face.

"Would you tell her I'll be at Yolanda's after school?"

"You'll be at Aunt Maggie's after school."

"But, Dad—"

"You heard me," he says. And I know there's no point in saying anything more about it.

7

Every Tuesday in Mrs. Taylor's language arts class we have poetry time, except I don't think Mrs. Taylor likes poetry very much. She certainly doesn't like the kind I like. We're supposed to bring in some lines from our favorite poets and talk about them. But if the poet isn't somebody she approves of, she cuts the discussion short. If you read from somebody like Walt Whitman or Edna St. Vincent Millay, she's happy.

This is the second Tuesday I've been at number 11. It's a stupid school. The first week, I wasn't prepared with any lines of poetry, so I started reciting "We Want No Irish Here." It's a song by Tommy Makem and a big favorite of my father's 'cause it's about the hard times the Irish had when they came to America. He likes to stand up and sing it at Gerrity's Tavern. He gets a big hand when he's done. I know most of it by heart. I know lots of my father's songs and poems by heart. Anyway, I could see Taylor starting to twitch before I finished the first stanza:

Our ship it docked in New York town.
And we took our bags ashore.
This was the land of the free, they said.
We'd see hard times no more.
But when we looked for work next day,
Wherever we'd appear,
The boss so proud, would shout out loud,
"We want no Irish here."

Taylor gave me this look like I was trying to spread communism or something and wouldn't let me recite the rest. I don't get what the big deal was. I mean Tommy Makem sang the song for President Kennedy at the White House, so it seems to me that if it's okay for the White House it ought to be okay for Mrs. Taylor's class. If I had Yolanda's nerve, I would have spoken up and told her that.

Today I figured I'd try something that wouldn't get her so itchy. So I recited a poem by Robert Frost, "Stopping by Woods on a Snowy Evening." Frost is the only poet my father likes who isn't Irish. He made an exception in his case 'cause President Kennedy likes him. Mrs. Taylor didn't mind that one. She let me finish the whole thing. It's the one about a man who stops in the woods to watch the snow fall, but he doesn't stay long because he's got "promises to keep." My father gets all sad when he recites it, but I don't think it's sad at all. Today it reminded me of Yolanda. She's like someone who has to keep going. She can't stop for long anywhere. She's got promises she's made to herself, things she's made up her mind to do.

I keep wondering how she talked her mother out of taking her to South Carolina. I picture how maybe she stood right up to her, hands on her hips, spoke her mind. I can't imagine standing up to my parents like that. I'm not even sure why I'm so afraid to do it. I don't know if it's even about fear. When I'm with them, I just lose track of who I am, what's important to me. Going to see Yolanda in the hospital is just about the only time I've ever disobeyed them. No wonder my father's so worried. I've always been such a goody two-shoes. Cait says so all the time. But I knew absolutely that it wasn't wrong for me to go see Yolanda. It was right. She was kind to me the day I ran away, and she wound up getting hurt because of it. Yolanda is my friend, and I'm going to see her whenever I want.

And when I see my mother tonight and she starts in about what happened at David's yesterday, that's exactly what I'm going to tell her. She can cry and moan all she wants about how I've disappointed her, but Yolanda is my friend. And that's never going to change. So she'd better get used to it.

Oh, God, it's my mother. She's sitting on Aunt Maggie's stoop. She never just sits out on the stoop, not unless it's a really hot summer night. And what's she doing home already on a Tuesday anyway? She's going to lace into me right here in the street. I'm not sure if she sees me yet, and I think of turning around, maybe hanging out in a store somewhere for a while. But I don't. I may as well get this over with. She sees me now, but she doesn't get up. She looks at me, then looks away. I'm not sure yet if this is going to be something from the martyr series or one of her boot-camp sergeant routines. I prefer the martyr bits. She looks toward the heavens like St. Theresa, holds her head in her hands for a time, and sighs. Of course, that usually signals the worst punishment, but it's worth it not to have to listen to the ranting.

I get to the stoop and stop in front of her. It's so odd to see her sitting here like this in the middle of the day. She's normally way too busy to be still. And living with Aunt Maggie, she's even busier, always wanting to be useful. She looks at me. I figure for sure she's going to start with "Look what you're turning into" or something like that, but she doesn't. She doesn't say anything for a minute.

"Sit down," she tells me, so I join her on the step. "Your father came to talk to me at work today."

I nod, but for the longest time she says nothing. We watch the kids coming home from school, hear some dogs barking. Next door, Mr. Callasurdo is leaving for work. He's a watchman at the bank on Tremont Avenue. He's got his gray uniform on, but he still looks like a farmer. The jacket is too short for him, and his hair is long and his neck thick. He's got his brown bag with his sandwiches in it. He waves at my mother and me. We wave back.

"You went to school today?" my mother says.

"Yes, I went to school." I sound defensive, but I can't blame her for checking.

Again she's quiet. Danny and Dennis Callahan come barreling out the door and leap over me onto the street. My mother can barely tolerate the Callahan boys. She thinks their mother is unfit. But that's mostly because her husband is long gone and she goes out on dates. She claims she doesn't leave the boys alone, says her sister is with them, but I know she does. "I don't know," my mother says, as if the Callahans are part of all of this somehow. "Maybe it's the right thing."

"What?"

"Your father wants us to move back in." She lets the words out with a deep breath, as if that's the only way she won't choke on them.

"With him, you mean?" although I'm almost sure that's what she means. I just don't know what else to say. I had a crazy thought that maybe he'd move out and let us live on Bryant Avenue again.

She nods. She's scratching at her hands. They can get really raw sometimes when she's worried. Only keeping busy keeps her from scratching.

"What does Aunt Maggie say?"

Mom shrugs. "I think it's time," she whispers. "Uncle Eddie's out all the time. Things aren't good here."

"Is there anywhere else we can ... I mean ... What about Uncle Brian?" That's my Dad's older brother. We haven't seen him in a couple of years, but we used to be close. He really likes my mom. But she shakes her head. We have nowhere else to go.

"I haven't got enough saved yet. It would take so long to get enough money together," she says. We've been living at Aunt Maggie's for more than two weeks. My mother doesn't make much at all. And we have to pay back all the bills we ran up at the apartment on Mapes Avenue. I think of the stuff people say about opportunities and making good for yourself. Seems to me the only people with opportunities are the ones who don't need them.

My mother looks so small here in the street, like when she's next to my dad, out of proportion to how important she is to us. When she's moving and doing, her energy makes her seem larger than she is. In fact, she's barely five feet tall. She wears high heels that click-clack on the street and on linoleum floors. My father is nearly six foot two, with broad shoulders and arms you can swing on. But it's not his size that makes him scary. It's not knowing what he'll do. When he's sober, he's kind of a lumbering bear, never quite sure of himself. But when he's drunk, it's like the stories of the ancient Irish warrior Cú Chulainn, transformed and distorted in his anger, ready to meet enemies so much bigger and meaner than he was. My dad gets larger, louder when he's angry. He doesn't hesitate at all. His face is grotesque. His tongue sticks out from the side of his mouth like a snake checking which way his prey has run. That's when you know he's about to lunge. But it's just us out there in front of him, no bigger than usual. One night when the chaos was all over, I found his shirt on a chair. I touched it. It was limp, soft flannel. I couldn't believe it was the same shirt, when just a little while before it had been filled with menace.

I'm afraid for my mother. She knows there's nothing but a promise between her and the next time he gets like that. "I'm sure Aunt Maggie and Uncle Ed will let us stay till you have enough." In fact, I'm not so sure at all. I've heard them arguing. The walls are thin, and when you're not wanted somewhere, the feeling fills the place like a smell. Normal people, people who have good jobs and good lives, believe it's all about choices. But some of us have 'em and some don't. Yolanda doesn't want to see that either, that her color will decide her choices for her. But I see it. That's the way it is for colored people, the same way it is for poor people, no matter what color they are. My mother can choose to stay here with her sister, like a beggar at the mercy of people who don't want her, or she can go back with my father, back where one night when the promise gets too tough for him to keep, there may be no mercy at all.

"And if we stay here, what can I expect from you?" she says, her voice so resigned it's almost a whisper. "More running away? More of this drinking?"

"I'm sorry, Mom," I tell her. But she looks away, as if my apology were no more meaningful than a toddler being sorry for a tantrum. My mom is playing with the clasp on her pocketbook, opening and closing it. The nervous repetition is like the timer on a game show or the ticking of a bomb. I remember standing with my mother once at a busy intersection. We'd just gotten off the B train and come up into the street. It was a pretty rough neighborhood, and she wasn't sure at all which way to go. She played with a button on her coat, opening and closing it, waiting for some clue to come. But it never did. She just took a chance, picked a direction, even if it got us lost. Just like she was going to do right now—and go back with my father.

9

I tried to hide it, but I was glad to leave Aunt Maggie's. So was Cait. We moved out this morning. Saturday, November 2, 1963. I wrote it really large in my journal first thing. When we were putting the last of the shopping bags into Uncle Ed's station wagon, Aunt Maggie started crying real hard, pleading with my mother to stay. Wait and see how things go, she kept saying. "It's not your fault, Maggie," my mother whispered, which seemed like a strange thing to say.

My mother put all the money she'd saved toward getting our things out of storage. My father came up with the rest. So the apartment is already starting to look like it did before. The living room seems almost like a living room again, and we've got all our clothes and the dishes and things. But being here feels so weird. We've been trying to figure out a way to fit together. It's like the zookeeper got mixed up and put the monkeys into the lion's cage and none of 'em is going to be foolish enough to sit still for long. So all morning, everybody just kept busy putting things back where they belong.

Around noon we realized we were all starving. Or I should say Owen realized it. He wanted to know when we were going to eat. My mom said she'd make hamburgers. It turned out there were no hamburger rolls in the house, but by then it was too late to change the menu. Owen and Liam didn't want any part of tuna sandwiches. That's when my father said he'd go to the store and get the rolls. The expression on my mother's face changed. Something in the whole room changed. Nobody said it, but everybody felt it. Once he left like that, there was no way to know what kind of shape he'd be in when he got back or what kind of damage he'd do. Most of my father's errands were a cover for stopping at Gerrity's Tavern. If they weren't, he wouldn't go in the first place. He'd make Cait or Liam go. Hearing Dad say he'd go to the store didn't exactly ease the tension in the place. Cait volunteered right away to go instead, but he waved her away, grabbed his jacket and headed for the door. He was eager to get out of there. I couldn't blame him. Putting a home back together when you're the one responsible for breaking it apart can't be too easy. There was no way to stop him. He was going to the store. We would just have to wait.

And we did. A half hour. An hour. Nearly an hour and a half. We ate the burgers on white bread. My mother flattened them out so they'd sort of fit. And now Owen, who soaks up the stress in our family like a sponge, is a wreck. Mom tells him to stop fidgeting all over the place and go outside and find his friends, but he won't. He keeps wandering from room to room, then settles into the kitchen every now and then. He's picking the stuffing out of a hole in the seat cushion of a kitchen chair.

I ate too fast and now I don't feel so good. The whole business is getting to me. I'm still working on the boxes piled up in the living room. They were packed by the moving men who evicted us, and the stuff was thrown in any old way— dishes with lampshades, sweaters with the shower curtain. I pull out the Monopoly game. The money and the houses are all over the bottom of the box, mixed with Owen's books and little army soldiers, and suddenly I don't want to bother looking for my clothes anymore. All I want to do is get the game organized. So I start separating the singles from the fives and the twenties, and I try to remember the last time we played it. I mean all of us. It has to be three years ago at least. But it was after dinner on a Saturday in the fall, like this one, and everybody was pressuring me to finish eating because they wanted to start the game. Mom had made meatloaf, which I hate. Liam had started winning pretty quickly. How everybody didn't know he was cheating I'll never under- stand. He was the banker, and he'd wink at me now and then, probably each time that he'd helped himself to a couple of hundred dollars when he was nowhere near passing Go.

My father had been drinking heavy all day, and he was pretty far gone when we sat down. He seemed okay, but he drank pretty much nonstop for the whole hour we played, and when the explosion came, it didn't surprise anybody. Owen had already left the game, pretending he had a stom- achache. I wanted to quit, too, but I had Marvin Gardens and Atlantic Avenue and the matching property was still free. If I got it, I could build houses, I'd have a chance to stay in the game. It's funny how when something awful is going to happen, you worry about trivial things, as if they were what mattered. Small problems feel good at times like that. I was counting everyone's houses and hotels. That's what I was doing when it started, so I didn't see what actually set Dad off. I only felt the table go flying away from me and the game board smacking me in the side of the head. Liam had landed hard on the floor in the money and the game pieces. "Get up," my father was screaming at him. "Get up before I give it to you again." Then Cait was screaming and my mother was pushing my father away. He knocked her down without even having to swing. Liam and my mother were such a handy set of punching bags: lightweight, low maintenance. And they'd bounce back up for more. Back then he didn't even have to duck any blows 'cause Liam was only fourteen and hadn't started going back at him yet.

No one's talking anymore. Not even Mom. She's sewing one of the cushions on the couch, and Liam is trying to get the picture on the television screen to stop jumping. Everybody hears it, the front door closing downstairs, his footsteps on the stairs. They stop, then start again. This isn't good. We all know it. Finally, we hear him outside the door, fumbling to get the key in the lock, but nobody goes to let him in.

"Bridget," Dad calls, but I can't tell how bad he is. I look at my mother. She's sitting up, rigid, clutching the pillow like a shield. Liam shakes his head at me as if to tell me not to move. Owen starts to cry.

"Bridget," he calls again, but this time the door opens. "Hey," he says, but still I can't tell what kind of shape he's in. He doesn't step in. He bends down instead and picks up something large. It takes me what feels like a long time to realize what it is. It's a lamp, the kind with a shade made of colored glass.

"Will you look at this?" he says. He doesn't feel the tension, has no idea what it's been like to wait for him. He's got his eyes locked on my mom, like he's someone who's won fair and square and now expects his prize. Mom looks as if she's trying to stand up, but she can't seem to get clear yet that everything's all right, that we're safe.

"Get a bulb from that lamp," Dad says to Liam, and Liam hurries to unscrew the light bulb from the lamp where my mother's been sewing and brings it over to him. Dad's on his hands and knees, reaching under the end table to plug in his find. "I took a walk up to Fordham Road. The fella in the grocery store—Smitty, you know Smitty, he's superintendent for that big new apartment building up there—he tells me they've just tossed out a gorgeous Tiffany lamp, in great shape. Can't be bothered with it just 'cause one little piece of color broke loose." And we can see, when he screws in the bulb and turns on the lamp, the diamond shape of white light escaping from the broken place among all the beautiful colors. My mother's chin trembles. She's going to cry. "Of course, I'm not sayin' it's the real thing, not a real Tiffany lamp, I mean. But it's a fine lamp just the same. Am I right, Bridie?" My mom is standing now, hypnotized, not by the lamp but by what he's done. "We can turn that part to the wall till I figure out a way to mend it," he says. She starts to cry. She's grateful, for the lamp, for our reprieve.

10

"You got it," Yolanda drawls. She sugars the words and the kid snaps them up like candy, wanting more, his eyes fixed on her face. That's not a voice I've heard Yolanda use that often. She turns the page for the boy and he gets back to work, sounding out the words as she points to them. He's only about eight. I can't tell if he's Negro or Puerto Rican. His hair is black and curly, but his skin is not very dark. When she corrects him, her diction is precise, with no accent that I can make out. The girl behind her, one of the other two kids Yolanda is working with, is getting fidgety, restless. She's supposed to be reading on her own, but instead she's pointing to pictures in a book her neighbor is reading, an older girl with a brooding face. Yolanda points to the story the younger one is supposed to be reading. "Are you reading, Brenda?" Yolanda asks her, but the little girl just shrugs. She wants Yolanda's attention, wants it to be her turn to read aloud again, to earn Yolanda's candy words.

Across the room, Yolanda's aunt Cheryl says something

I can't hear to the boys she's working with and then stands and comes over to me. "Would you mind reading with her for a little bit?" Cheryl whispers, motioning toward the little girl. "We're almost done here."

"Sure," I say. Cheryl walks me over to Brenda, and I slip into an empty chair nearby.

"Brenda, this is Fiona," Cheryl tells her. "She's going to read with you for a while." Before the girl can offer an opinion for or against the idea, Cheryl has already pulled her, chair and all, back a bit from where Yolanda is reading with the boys. The girl who was next to Brenda is happy to be rid of her. She sinks quickly back into her book, sliding into a slouch, the only comfort the straight-backed chair will allow.

"Ona?" Brenda says to me. "Your name is Ona?"

"*Fi*ona," I tell her, and she looks at me as if I must be making it up, that these odd syllables can't really be anyone's name. But she keeps herself from saying that. She tries my name out again, maybe wondering if this is just another of the grown-up world's many pranks.

The book she's reading is handmade, with a text pieced together from words cut mostly from second-grade readers, like a ransom note for Dick and Jane. Brenda already knows the words. I point to the first word at the top of the page and she rattles off the rest of the sentence like a guide repeating a tired bit of history for a new set of tourists. I tell her to keep going and she does, this time with a little more expression. The story is about a boy named Roy who has wandered after his dog into a used-car lot. The boy walks between cars, calling his dog, and on each page we turn, another photograph of a car has been pasted into the margin. When Brenda says *Chevy* instead of *Chevrolet,* I know she's reciting and not reading, so I make her go back to the word. She has no trouble with it, but she makes a show of putting her finger beneath each syllable and sounding them out carefully. I compliment her, and she says thank you and looks at me. She's got eyes as dark as Yolanda's, but they're big and round and demanding.

"You have a million freckles," she tells me. I nod. "Did you get them all at once?" she wants to know.

I'm about to laugh, but she really wants an answer. "I don't know," I say, "but in the summer I get even more."

"But won't your face run out of room some day?" This time I can't help giggling. "Don't worry," she says. "Maybe your face will get bigger."

I turn the page, and just as Roy finds his dog eating something from the hand of a huge man in dirty overalls, Cheryl tells everyone it's time to wrap things up. You'd think the kids would take this as good news. I mean, here it is, a gorgeous Saturday afternoon in early November, and a dozen kids are indoors doing schoolwork on what has to be a day off for school kids all over the civilized world. But they don't. Nobody slams his book closed. Nobody leaps for the door. They want to hang around. Some of the little ones want hugs, and Cheryl and Yolanda oblige. Brenda doesn't make any move to hug me, but she gives me a big smile as she's leaving. Whatever goes on here, it's not like any class I've ever had. Two older girls, who've been working in the kitchen—they look like they could be seniors—come out and hand some papers to Cheryl. They put their coats on and talk to her about which days they can come during the week. They have jobs to go to.

Yolanda helps the kids gather up the books and papers to put away. She gives me a quick wave, a little embarrassed. She didn't know I'd get here so early. I didn't know it either. I was going to walk here. That's what I told Yolanda on the phone. She suggested three o'clock, but my dad gave me a ride, so I got here twenty minutes earlier.

Yolanda and I have a lot to catch up on. I haven't seen her since Monday, the day we left the hospital, and with everything that's happened, that seems like a lifetime ago. She doesn't have to go to South Carolina. I know that much, anyway. But on the phone she didn't seem as happy about it as I thought she'd be. There's something else bothering her. I hope it's nothing really bad, 'cause it would be nice if things could just be good for us for a change. My mom was actually smiling at my dad when he got the lamp set up, and she made him a huge hamburger and didn't even yell at him for forgetting the hamburger rolls. And when I asked if I could go to Yolanda's, she didn't react as if I ought to be excommunicated. I don't mean she liked the idea, and I don't mean everything is what you'd call normal—normal in my family is going to take a few more generations—but my father bringing back that lamp took the insanity down to semipro level.

Once most of the kids are gone, Yolanda and I head upstairs to her room, and she drills me with questions the whole way, but mostly just about having my stuff back from storage. "My dad's taking off from work on Monday to see if he can get me registered for school."

"You mean number 6?" She's really happy to hear it.

"My mother called the school yesterday. They said it's okay. It will take a while for my records to catch up, but I can start anyway."

Yolanda smiles. "So tell me already. How is it so far?" She means at home, with my parents back together.

"It's pretty strange. But nobody's hospitalized yet, so who knows? Maybe it'll last this time."

"Must be nice to have your stuff back," she says, opening the door to her room.

"I found my favorite top," I tell her, pulling at the blue sweater I'm wearing. "I forgot I had it." We plop on the bed as if we've been doing hard labor all day. As soon as I feel the mattress under me, I realize how tired I am. We got up so early this morning to unpack. And everything's been so tense all day. I feel my arms and legs untighten as I look up at Yolanda's posters.

"Do you think it might last?" Yolanda says.

I have no idea. But I know Yolanda doesn't want to hear that. She's always thinking if you have a plan, you're safe. All I can tell her is it's okay for now.

"But he hasn't been drinking, right?" she says.

I tell her how scared we were today when he went out

and about how he came back with the lamp and how pleased my mother seemed to be.

"Well, it's a start," Yolanda says. She doesn't push me to agree, doesn't ask any more questions about my folks. "You were really good with Brenda," she says.

"You think so?" I tell her. I like hearing her say it.

"She's one of our toughest, believe it or not. She's a cute kid, but she gets restless really fast, and without much warning she can get herself into a state."

"A state?"

"Kind of like a low-grade tantrum. That's her biggest problem in school. If she doesn't get attention, she goes into orbit and she winds up getting sent out of the class. She's missed so much work, they may put her back in first grade if she doesn't settle down. They only promoted her on the condition that she catches up and straightens out."

"That's too bad. She seems pretty bright."

"Oh, she is. Her problem is she has no control. And she doesn't take to everyone, either. She liked you."

"You think so? She did smile at me when she was leaving."

"Definitely. Cheryl tries to work with her, but it never goes well. It's because Cheryl is strictly business. Brenda wants mostly attention, not instruction."

Yolanda doesn't say any more about Brenda. We listen to other sounds in the house. It's quiet, seems like all the kids have left. I hear Cheryl's voice coming in and out, maybe on the phone downstairs.

"Where's your mom?" I say.

Yolanda lets out a breath, like she knew this was coming, but her answer doesn't come right away, so I wait. "She went to see some friends of hers. To say good-bye."

"Good-bye?"

"Yeah, 'cause when she leaves this time, she's not coming back for a while."

"Leaves? I thought you weren't going to South Carolina."

"I'm not. But she is."

"What? Without you?"

Yolanda nods.

"When you said you didn't have to go, I just thought … I thought …" Then I shut up, because you don't have to be Einstein to figure out how this must make Yolanda feel.

"She really wants to live there," Yolanda says.

I want to ask why her mom would want to live anywhere but with Yolanda, but I don't.

"She's getting married. He's got family there, two sons, a lot younger than me. I heard her tell Cheryl she wants to do it right this time."

"Right?"

"She's going to have a baby. His baby. And this time she wants a proper family." Yolanda's parents must have gotten a divorce when she was pretty young. That must be what her mother means by "doing it right."

"A baby," I say. "Geez."

"She wasn't going to have it," Yolanda says. I don't understand what she means. Yolanda turns to me. "An abortion," she says. I just stare at her, dumbfounded. "Haven't you ever heard of having an abortion?"

I hear her, but I can't speak. Everybody knows abortion is a really, really serious sin. You go straight to hell for it. No excuses. When my aunt Maggie got pregnant right after she had Maureen, the doctor said she shouldn't be pregnant again. It was too soon. He said she needed to have an abortion, but Father McMahon said she'd be excommunicated. Uncle Ed said the hell with Father McMahon and the hell with the Church, but she went ahead and had the baby. She was so sick the whole time, and when Eddie was born, he almost died. So did she. It was terrible, but she wouldn't dare have an abortion. I don't tell Yolanda this, 'cause I'm not sure how things are with Protestants. My grandmother says anything goes with them. "Isn't that against the law?" I say instead.

"That's why she went to South Carolina back in June. They know somebody down there."

I think of terrible, dark back rooms and cold, mean people. Baby killers. I could never go to such a place. I'd be brave like my aunt Maggie. But I don't say that. "So what happened? How come she changed her mind?" I figure it didn't have much to do with being worried about getting into heaven.

"She doesn't think I know about the abortion stuff. All she told me was that she loves Andy and they want to get married. And that they're going to have a family."

"Did she tell you she's going to have a baby?"

"It's not exactly something she can keep a secret any-more. She's got a belly already." I don't say anything. "Cheryl is mad at her. My mom says she doesn't understand. She says it's her chance to have the kind of life she wants."

"She told you that?"

"No. I heard them talking. Then she asked if I wanted to come down there with her." The way Yolanda says this sounds like she's trying hard to believe that her mother really wants her.

"What did you tell her?"

"I told her I couldn't go."

"And?"

Yolanda swallows hard. "She said she understood. She says I'm big now and can make up my own mind."

It's the most awful thing I've ever heard. Going off to start a new life and leaving people behind like they're some-thing you can scrape off your shoe. I mean it's not like she's in my mother's situation. Nobody was beating up Yolanda's mom. Why can't she start over right here in the Bronx, where Yolanda can be with her?

We're so quiet that the street sounds make their way into the room—a truck lumbering to a stop, a boy shouting to his friends. I want to say something helpful, but I don't know what it should be. Maybe I should go along with Yolanda's act, pretend with her that it's not such a big thing that her mother's going away. I say "I'm sorry" the way I hear grown-ups say it at funerals, when there's nothing else you can say. Yolanda makes a sound, like she's going to burst into tears.

It scares me, so I touch her hand. "Oh," she says, and I don't know what's going to come next or what I'll do if she really breaks down. But the touch changes everything, brings her to her senses, and she coughs instead. She turns to me, and the look on her face is different, like she trusts me. It feels like a reward, like I've earned something few people get from Yolanda. "Thank you, Fiona," she says. And I nod. I want to hug her, but you can't do that with Yolanda. She doesn't like goofy stuff like that.

She gets up and sits on the edge of the bed, like we're late for something, like it's way past time to move on. "You should work with Brenda," she says. She's on her feet now. I'm not sure what she means. She looks at me to see what I think of the idea. "You should tutor her. You'd be good with her."

It takes a second to sink in, but when it does, I smile. I felt good when I was helping Brenda, like she thought I was important, like maybe I could *be* important. "You think so?" I say.

"Let's talk to Cheryl," she says, and heads out the door. I'm up and following her down the stairs before she has time to change her mind.

11

It's not as if I was expecting a welcoming committee to greet me with the school band; a quick nod would have worked for me. My dad and I sat on the bench in the main office yesterday for almost twenty minutes, waiting for the principal to see us, and during that time at least three kids that were in my classes here last year came in—and saw me. No, make that pretended not to see me. Kathy Campbell stared at me like she was waiting for an explanation, but when I said hello, she just looked away. Natalie Brauer practically stepped on my feet, but I got no more notice than a dropped pencil. After my father and I got the happy news that I could report to classes right away, things got even worse. I had to walk in at the tail end of language arts, and while Mrs. Cornwallis made an exasperated to-do about finding me a book and a seat, everybody else whispered and stared and got a case of mass amnesia when old Cornwallis trilled, "Class, we all remember Fiona O'Doherty, don't we?" Nobody was ready to admit to it. "Fiona was with us last year, weren't you, Fiona?"

I thought about insisting she had me confused with some other Mick, but who cared anyway. The old bat could at least have learned how to pronounce my name this time around.

I searched the rows for black faces, hoping Yolanda might be in the room, but no such luck. She wasn't in the next class either, but in history, the class before lunch, she finally showed. I was presenting my admission slip to Mr. Margolin, who, as far as I can tell, still hasn't had his jacket dry-cleaned, when Yolanda slipped in just after the bell. She walked to the back and chose a desk that had another empty one next to it, and she waved me over. I turned to Margolin to see if it was all right for me to sit there and he nodded. Margolin's the kind of grown-up who doesn't make an issue out of things that don't matter, things like sitting in alphabetical order.

Margolin opened up with a pop quiz on the Civil War, which he said I could skip, but I took it anyway. We exchanged papers for grading and Yolanda marked mine. I didn't do that badly. She marked it fair and square, too. Yolanda never cheats, not even the littlest bit. She's too proud. Margolin let the class use the last five minutes to start the homework, and Yolanda and I passed notes back and forth. She wanted to know if my parents were going to let me tutor. I said they were okay with it—my mom thinks I might still have a shot at redemption—but they didn't like me coming home after dark. "We'll figure something out," Yolanda wrote. I didn't doubt it.

When the bell rang, we headed for the cafeteria, talking nonstop about my classes that morning, about how pleased

Cheryl was that I was going to help with the tutoring. When we finished eating, kids were giving us looks. White kids just don't hang out with colored kids; but I was so happy to see Yolanda and we had so much to tell each other that it felt perfectly normal for us to be together. I guess I just forgot. We decided not to go out into the courtyard after we ate, the way all the kids do, because even though we didn't say it, we knew we'd have to separate. Out there the colors don't mix; neither do the sexes or the grades. White eighth-grade girls stay with the white eighth-grade girls and that's that. So Yolanda and I stayed in the cafeteria and talked.

Mary Hennessy, Terry Mazzarachio, and Kathy Campbell turned out to be in my math class after lunch. They pretended not to know me. Yolanda is in the class, too. But if you so much as hiccup in Miss Cassidy's class, she decides you have a bad attitude. So we didn't talk much for the rest of the day or even after school because I had to get home. I promised my mom I'd unpack the last of the boxes and put as much of the stuff away as I could.

Today was my second day, Tuesday, November 5, and school was pretty much the same, with the dirty looks we got at lunch and the other kids treating me like I have a Martian blood type. I tried to be friendly. My mom told me last night that people treat you the way you treat them. She said maybe I was acting like I didn't want to be friendly. I figured maybe that was true, because I was so nervous, so this morning in language arts I said hi, real friendly, to Mary Hennessy and asked her if she had any trouble with the math homework. I used to help her with her homework sometimes last year. She has a real hard time with math. So does Yolanda. "Those exercises were a pain," I said. "Did you get them all?" She pursed her lips at me, as if to say "what a stupid question." "Cassidy said it's going to be on the test Friday," I said, not ready to give up yet.

Mary gave me this I-know-something-you-don't-know kind of laugh and looked at Kathy Campbell. "Mary aces Cassidy's tests," Kathy announced.

I didn't say it, but the look on my face did: "Since when?"

"Yeah, I've got a 91 average this marking period," Mary said.

"Wow," I said. "I should be asking *you* for help." All I got was this look, like maybe I should go clap erasers on my ears or something, and a grunt. I think my mother needs to update her take on human relations. These girls are just plain nasty.

That doesn't stop me from wishing I could be one of them. I see them together, whispering and giggling, with their neat outfits and their perfect hair—all blonds and browns—and I want to be part of things. They talk about going shopping on Tremont Avenue or listening to Beach Boys or Bobby Vinton records at each other's houses. None of them looks like she just stayed up all night waiting for her mother to get back from the emergency room. Nobody looks like she's ever had to skip a meal. They don't have a single thing to be ashamed of. Just once I'd like to see what that feels like, to be one of them—one of the girls they're not nasty to. I tried again in second-period science with Terry Mazzarachio, but the results weren't any better. She said hi back, but when the class had to separate into groups for discussion, she made sure she wasn't in mine. Yolanda and I ate lunch together, but we couldn't come up with a solution for getting me home from tutoring. Cheryl could get me home on Wednesdays, but that was the only day of the week she didn't have SNCC meetings or work to go to.

After our last class, Yolanda said she'd wait for me in the schoolyard after school, but she's not here yet. The kids are streaming out of the building, so I'm watching pretty carefully. I hear David call my name. He's standing by the gate, a bag of books slung over his shoulder, wearing a leather jacket. He looks so cool, so like … I don't know … older.

"Hey," he says when I turn toward him.

"David," I say, and walk over to him. He's smiling.

"I figured you might be back here by now," he says.

"How did you know … I …"

"Cheryl told my mother. You know how it goes." I nod, afraid of how much he might know about me and my family now. "So what's it like being back?" he says.

I shrug.

"Is Yolanda in any of your classes?"

I tell him about history and math.

"Good," he says, and I notice Kathy Campbell and Mary Hennessy coming across the schoolyard. They see me and they whisper—about something pretty important from the looks of it.

"Listen, Fiona …," David says, but he stops, like he doesn't really know how to say what he has to say. "There's something I want to tell you," he says, but it doesn't come out.

"What, David?" I say. Behind him Natalie Brauer is standing with Kathy and Mary now, and I'll be darned if they're not all staring at me—at both of us.

"I want to apologize," he says, but I'm distracted by the spontaneous gathering of the in-crowd, all of them focused on us.

"Apologize?" I say.

"You know," he says, "for last week. I got you two in a lot of trouble. I got myself in a lot of trouble, too."

"It wasn't your fault," I say, waving off the apology.

"The wine was a bad idea."

"For me at least," I say.

David laughs. "Why? 'Cause you blew your cover?" he says, and I remember the CIA business about the freckles on my arm.

The in-crowd is approaching us now, and I'm expecting the cold shoulder, but instead I hear my name chimed. "Hi, Fiona," they say with tongues coated in honey. I stare at their smiles, stunned. "Hi, David," they trill in a pitch reserved for boys and suckers. It's David's attention they want. I just happen to be in his orbit. They sway past, slow enough to do a graceful about-face if he decides to invite one, but he doesn't. He just waves. But even that's enough to get them giggling. He rolls his eyes.

"So what have you and Yolanda been up to?" he says.

"Her aunt Cheryl wants me to help with the tutoring they do after school."

"Great."

"Problem is, I don't have a way to get home, and my mom says it ends too late to walk."

"Doesn't the number 3 bus go that way?"

"She's not keen on buses either." That's not true. It's just that she may not have the money for two bus rides a week. "There's Yolanda," I say, waving, though she already sees us.

David waves, too. "So what days do you need a ride home?"

"Mondays and Fridays."

"I bet my mom could take you home."

"Really?"

"Hey," Yolanda says when she reaches us. "What's this? Alumni week?"

David grins. "I came by to apologize for getting us all into trouble last week."

"You call that trouble?" she says. "That wouldn't even get a mention in my neighborhood."

David laughs. So do I. "It can't hold a candle to getting hospitalized," he says, "but Cheryl didn't look too pleased and neither did Mr. O'Doherty."

Yolanda laughs, as if picturing them again. "Well, thanks for the apology. But no harm done."

"How's the rib?"

"Much better. No problem at all really."

"Good."

Yolanda looks at her watch. "Listen, I gotta go. Cheryl's going to be waiting."

"Mrs. Silverman might be able to give me a ride home from your place," I tell Yolanda.

"Really?" she says to David. She's pleased.

"I'll ask her," David says. "She'll probably do it. Another notch on her do-gooder belt."

"That's great," Yolanda tells him, then turns to me. "Okay, then, tomorrow for sure, 'cause Aunt Cheryl will take you home."

"But don't you think we should wait till David talks to his mother?"

"Are you kidding? This boy knows how to work it. I gotta go. I'll see you tomorrow. 'Bye, David," she says and moves quickly down the street.

"So you headed home?" David says.

"Yup."

"I'll walk with you." We head up 174th Street, the late afternoon sun bright in our faces, and so all I see at first are silhouettes. Still, there's no mistaking who it is. A block ahead of us and across the street, the in-crowd is standing outside Katz's Deli, minus only their spyglasses.

12

Figure this one out. Kathy Campbell and Mary Hennessy were nice to me today. It happened first thing, in language arts class. The bell hadn't rung yet and Cornwallis was busy putting sentences on the board. She starts off each class with a torture treatment: she writes three sentences on the board and we have to diagram them. I had to pass Kathy and Mary to get to my desk, and they said hello. I was stunned, but I said hello back. Then it got even weirder. Mary said she liked my sweater. We both know that Mary wouldn't be caught dead in this sweater. I mean it's an okay sweater. It's an aqua-blue turtleneck, but it was Cait's sweater and you can tell it's seen some action. It has pills on it, and the bottom's kind of stretched. Even when it was new it wouldn't have fit me right. Two years ago, when Cait wore it, she had more to put into it than I do. So I don't know why Mary and Kathy decided it was okay not to ignore me this morning, but I know for sure it's not because they like what I'm wearing. I think David's visit yesterday pulled me up a rung on the social ladder.

When the class was over, they walked me halfway to my second-period class. I have to admit, I liked it. They were making fun of Cornwallis and they were pretty funny. Then in second period, Terry Mazzarachio and another girl I don't know that well, named Ruth, told me I could be on their lab team. We don't have much of a lab. I mean we don't really cut anything up. Mostly Mrs. Woken just holds up jars of organs and animal guts and we look at pictures of where the parts used to be. It's all pretty gross, but it'll be great not to have to look at the pictures with smelly Bud Wilson and his partner Arny. They're the only other lab team that still had room for one more. Terry and Ruth were friendly after class ended, too. Ruth even asked me what I was doing after school. She said sometimes they get together at her place or at Mary's. I said I was busy today, but maybe we could do it another day. They acted like that might happen. So by the time I met up with Yolanda after school, I was feeling good, strange but good.

Everything just seems to be working out. Mrs. Silverman called me last night and said she'd take me home from tutoring on Mondays and Fridays. David was right. His mother sounded happy to do it. I'm still short of breath from how fast Yolanda and I walked to her house after school. She wanted to give Cheryl some time with me before the kids get here, so she could explain what I'll be doing and show me the books they have. They have a lot of them, an odd collection. Some are homemade ones, like the one I was reading with Brenda, but there are old editions of readers from public schools, the ones that get thrown out. They're pretty beat up. I never had a new textbook in school. I didn't think the books were ever replaced, at least not until they just about disintegrated or somebody threw one out a window. That's probably what happened to these.

When Brenda arrives, Cheryl explains to her that she's going to be working with me. She shrugs, tells Cheryl she wants the desk chair today. The desk chair is a relic, the kind where the seat is attached to the desk and the desk has a lid that lifts up. Cheryl says okay, just for today. I get the feeling she doesn't want to set Brenda off by refusing. I let her pick out a new book to start, like Cheryl told me to, and I pull up a chair to be next to her. She has a white blouse on, most of which is no longer tucked into a gray skirt that was probably pleated this morning but isn't anymore. She gets right down to business, maybe wanting to show me her stuff, 'cause she sails through three pages about a girl who can't decide what present to get for her mom. It's pretty dumb, not nearly as good as the homemade book, and I think she's read it many times already.

On page 4, she stops, says she has a question. She wants to know what school I go to. I tell her I go to school with Yolanda. That's the mostly white school, she says. She's right, but I don't say anything. She says I must be in eighth grade like Yolanda and I tell her I am. I try to get her back to the story, but she wants to know if I have sisters or brothers. I tell her I do, and she wants to know their names.

"I'll tell you their names, but then we have to get back to reading, okay?"

"Okay."

"Their names are Owen, Catharine—but we call her Cait—and Liam."

"Liam?"

"Yes."

"That's a funny name. How come your family has such funny names?"

"They're Irish names."

"So you're Irish?" I nod. "Have you ever seen one of those lepers?"

"Lepers? What do you mean?"

"You know. The fairies with the funny hats on."

I laugh. "You mean *leprechauns*."

"Leprechauns. Right," she says.

"They're not real," I tell her. She looks at me, not ready to agree. I point to the first word on page 4.

"'Last year Susan had gotten her mother an apron,'" Brenda reads, barely having to look at the words. She's silent for a second, looking at my chin. "Do you go to the big church?"

"You mean St. Thomas Aquinas? Yes."

"My grandma says they do conjuring in there."

"Conjuring?"

"You know. Black magic," she says, looking at me as if she's not sure she wants to hear the details if it's true.

"Don't be silly," I say, even though she's got a point. Except the only thing the incense and the genuflecting and the mumbo jumbo really conjure up is guilt. The Church never

runs short of things you can go to hell for. And some of 'em—
like eating meat on Friday—are so ordinary you wouldn't
know you were that bad a person unless they told you.

I point to the page, and she reads the next sentence but
then stops again. "I don't get what this girl's all upset about,"
she says. "So what if she gets her mother the same present her
friend gets *her* mother. It's stupid." I can't argue with her.

"Want to write your own story?" I say.

She looks at me, then glances over at Cheryl as if she's
not sure that's allowed. "You mean make one up?"

"Yeah, maybe we can make a storybook like the one you
were reading the last time I was here."

"Okay," she says, excited. I get some paper from the shelf
behind us and she inches closer to me, almost like a snuggle.

"How do you want to start?" I say. She holds the pencil
tight, and her other hand opens and closes, as if she's
pumping gas for her brain.

"Once upon a time," she says.

"Once upon a time? Don't you want to write a story about
real life? Like the one we read about Roy and his dog?"

"No. I don't want it to be real life."

"Oh, you want a fairy tale?" I ask. She nods. "Okay. Go
ahead."

She begins to write, but she writes the numeral 1.

"No, you have to write the word," I tell her.

"I don't know how to spell it."

"I can spell it for you. O-n-c-e." She writes each letter
very large and very slowly as I say them, and she's never sure

of the right place on the line to start them. The *e* comes out upside down, so I show her how to do that one, but I don't correct the others. She's eager to get into the story.

When she gets the whole line written, she blurts out the rest. "There was a lonely old man who was running out of turnips."

"Is that what he liked to eat? Only turnips?"

"Yes, and he lived all alone in the jungle. ..."

"Are there turnips in the jungle?"

"Of course," she says, looking at me as if I'm hopeless. "But he's old now and he has eaten so many that there are hardly any left. And he searches far and wide, but he can't find any. And he won't hunt the animals because he loves them and they love him."

"Wow," I say. "He's really got a problem. That's a great story."

She starts to write again, but she's got so much to get down that I offer to write for her while she dictates. It's hard for me not to laugh at some of what she's saying, but I manage. We come to a part where the old man finds a lemon tree, and she stops. I don't think she knows what she wants to happen.

"What's his name?" I ask her.

"He doesn't have a name. He's like a tree or a wild animal. They don't have names."

"I see."

"You even have freckles on your hands," she says, and touches the back of my hand.

"Yup," I say, and realize we're smiling at each other. "Want to put the story aside for a while? Let's read at least one story from the shelf today."

"Okay," she says, and we go back to see how Susan will solve the problem of what to buy her mother. Brenda has more patience with it now, although it's even dumber than it was when it started. Who cares what she buys her mother? In real life, in mine at least, the story wouldn't be about what to buy her mother; it would be about how she was going to pay for it.

Before we can finish, we hear Cheryl's chair scrape against the thin carpet and we know it's time for everyone to finish up. Brenda knows where the reader belongs and returns it to the same spot on the shelf. I ask Cheryl if there's a place we can keep things till Friday, a folder or something.

"Did you work on penmanship?" Cheryl says.

"Not really, we were writing a story." Cheryl looks at the papers and back at me, and I wonder if I did something wrong.

"Fiona says my story is really good," says Brenda.

"I bet it is," Cheryl says, seeming pleased now, and I breathe a sigh of relief. "Are you going to read it to us when you finish?"

"We're going to make a storybook," says Brenda. "We'll read it when it's a book."

"Well, that will be even better," Cheryl tells her. She turns to tend to two boys who've been tugging at her shirt, and I get started helping Yolanda put the room back in order.

"We have to put the chairs away tonight. There's company coming."

"Company?"

"Mostly my mom's friends. A few relatives."

"Is it a birthday or something?" As soon as I say it, I feel so stupid, because I realize what it must be for.

"No. My mom's leaving in the morning."

"I see."

I follow Yolanda to the enclosed front porch that separates the living room from the front door, and I hand her some folding chairs while she tucks them into a corner. "You can stay for dinner if you want. Roast beef. It's just us for dinner. The rest of the folks won't be here till after. For the cake." She makes the invitation sound casual, but I know it isn't. She doesn't want to do this alone, this farewell thing. I want to stay, but I'm not sure what I'm going to tell my folks.

"I'll have to call home," I tell her.

"Sure," she says, but she sounds as if I've told her no.

"I'd really like to stay. I just better let them know, okay?"

Yolanda nods and points to the phone on the hall table, but I hesitate. I wish I didn't have to call from there, right where everybody can hear me. "There's another one, at the top of the stairs in the hall," she says.

I go up. It's almost dark outside now, and there's no light on in the hall, but it's easy to spot. I pick up the huge black receiver and dial the number.

"Hello?" It's Cait.

"Hi," I say. "It's me."

"Everything okay? You got a ride, right? You know Mom don't want you—"

"I have a ride. It's not that."

"What, then?"

"I won't be home for dinner."

"What do you mean?"

"I'm going to eat at a friend's house."

"Yolanda's?" she says, her voice up now.

"What difference does it make?"

"You know what the difference is. Fiona, come on. The tutoring is one thing, but she's going to go nuts when she hears this." Cait's voice has that tone in it, like I'm really putting her on the spot.

"Cait, her mom is leaving tomorrow. The dinner is to say good-bye."

"You mean for South Carolina? It's tomorrow?"

"Yeah. This is the last time she'll see her till who knows when. I gotta stay." Cait doesn't answer. "Please, Cait. She's my friend."

"Can't you pick friends who are Italian or Polish?"

"That's so dumb. I can't help that she's a Negro. Neither can she."

Nobody says anything for what seems like a long time. "Okay," Cait says. "I'll figure something out."

"Thanks," I tell her.

"You got a ride though, right?"

"Cheryl's driving me."

"Okay. Listen, when you get home, no matter what I say, you just nod. Understand?"

"I understand."

"And for heaven's sake, stay sober."

I laugh, 'cause I know she's teasing.

"Okay, but just for tonight," I say. "See you later."

I hang up and swirl around to rush back downstairs, but before I'm halfway down, I see Yolanda, sitting at the bottom of the stairs, and I can tell from the look on her face that she's heard everything I said.

13

I have no idea what to say to Yolanda when she gets like this. She won't face reality. A lot of white people I know—especially the ones in my family—just don't like colored people, and they don't like white people being with colored people unless they have no choice. Look at television. Look at the movies. When do you ever see Negroes and whites together? I saw a movie once with Sidney Poitier and Tony Curtis, but they were tied together at the ankles 'cause they broke away from a chain gang. That's the only reason a black man and a white man are allowed to become friends in a movie, when they're forced to.

But Yolanda acts like I should be able to change the way people feel. She looks at me like I'm a coward, just because I don't scream and yell every time my family gives me a hard time that Yolanda's colored. There's not a lot I can do to change their minds. I mean I'm not a one-man march. I'm just trying to keep my mother from blowing her top, which is what she does when I mention Yolanda's name. And if that means I have to lie sometimes, then I have to lie. I can't stage a civil rights demonstration every time I want to do something with Yolanda.

I get to the bottom of the stairs and Yolanda stands up. I brace myself for the scolding, but it doesn't come. She just gestures toward the kitchen, signaling for me to follow her there. The kitchen smells like all systems are go, and Cheryl is by the sink cutting a kind of vegetable I've never seen before. My mom doesn't get involved in much more than potatoes and corn. Cabbage we have only once a year 'cause my mother hates the smell of it.

"Well, here they are," says Cheryl, and her smile lifts Yolanda right out of the ornery mood she's in, "Yolanda and our fine new tutor."

"I knew she'd be good at it," Yolanda says, grabbing at the I-told-you-so.

"And you were right," says Cheryl.

"Last year Mrs. McKenna put Richie Crenshaw in a reading group all by himself," Yolanda tells her. "Remember that, Fiona?"

"Yes," I say.

"Mostly because he was dumb as a stump and none of the other groups was slow enough for him to keep up with. And Miss Einstein here used to finish way ahead of everyone else, so she started reading with him. Was a good thing, too, 'cause otherwise Crenshaw would probably still be sitting in that corner, trying to get past the title page."

The truth is our class had a shot at winning a free library

period at the end of the semester, but only if everybody finished reading the unit, including Crenshaw. I couldn't stand the though of us losing 'cause of him. And it didn't look as if McKenna cared. She treated our reading period like free time for her to mark papers instead of helping kids like Crenshaw. I felt bad for him.

"Some people just have a natural talent," says Cheryl.

"Yup," Yolanda declares. "Fiona's a scribbler, too."

Cheryl laughs and explains to me that that's what she has called Yolanda since she was small and used to bring home ten books at a time from the library.

"At first, I thought Fiona might be slipping Brenda candy under the desk," Cheryl says.

"Whatever works," Yolanda laughs.

"Did you call your folks about staying for dinner?" Cheryl asks me.

I nod and Cheryl tells us we'll need a folding chair from the front porch. I head down the hall to get it, feeling a little surprised at how comfortable I am, so at home. The front porch is completely dark and I feel for the light. I flip it on and reach for one of the chairs we just put away. As I slide it toward me, I hear the front door opening. The cool air rushes in, and a woman slips in quickly, eager to be inside.

"Well, hello," she says. Her smile is so big, like joy from a loudspeaker, and her deep black eyes take me in like a hug, like I'm just the one she was looking for. I can't stop looking at her. "You must be Fiona," she says. I nod, but I'm not sure my "hi" is loud enough for her to hear. She unbuttons her loose coat, and I can see how large her stomach is. Her skin is dark, maybe even darker than Yolanda's, and so smooth across her cheeks that it looks like chocolate frosting on an ice-cream bar. Her nose and her mouth are wide and full, and I can't help staring. "I've heard about you." I nod and she smiles again. "How did you like the tutoring?"

The question makes me stop staring. "I like it. It was good."

"Did they give you Brenda?" I nod and she laughs, as if she's in on some mischief.

"She was fine, though."

"Good, good," she says, and touches the top of her tummy absently, the way I remember Aunt Maggie doing when she was pregnant. "I'm glad you're here," she says, but she's not smiling anymore. She moves closer to me and leans in, as if whatever is next should be just between us. "Yolanda's going to need a good friend." She says it like it's something she wants us to agree on, something I shouldn't take lightly.

"I know," I say, and she turns slowly toward a noise inside the house that I didn't hear. Yolanda's standing in the hall. Mrs. Baker steps inside and drops her coat on a chair. She walks up to Yolanda and says her name, like a question, but Yolanda doesn't answer. Mrs. Baker reaches around to hold her anyway. Her tummy makes the embrace awkward. Yolanda doesn't put her arms around her in return. But Mrs. Baker doesn't let go. She just keeps holding her, saying her name, like an incantation. I wish Yolanda would hug her back, but she won't. The leaving has to start for them sometime, and for Yolanda, it already has.

14

It's happening. It's actually happening. I've got friends, friends who are some of the most popular girls in school. We're all in Mary Hennessy's living room now, all six of us—Mary, Kathy, Natalie, Ruth, Terry, and me. We were up in Mary's bedroom, but the phone keeps ringing so much that her mother told us to come downstairs 'cause she's too busy to keep answering it. Mary's mother doesn't work and she's only got one kid, so I'm not sure what she's busy at. She has put out a huge bowl of M&M's for us, and there's a basket full of fruit on the counter. The last time I had M&M's, we were going to the movies and my mother didn't want to have to pay the price for candy from the candy counter, so she splurged and got a bag at the grocery store. She had to hide it in her coat pocket so the usher wouldn't make a stink about it. Even at Yolanda's last night, they had so much food, so much dessert, it felt like Thanksgiving. None of the other girls seems to find this particularly extravagant, so I play it cool and act like it's perfectly normal to have candy and fruit for no occasion at all.

I like it better down here. Upstairs Mary was playing a Connie Francis record for almost half an hour. It looked to me like I was the only one who was going to be sick from it. I like it better when the TV is on. It keeps the focus off me. For a while upstairs, I thought Terry Mazzarachio was going to drag out a polygraph and strap me to it. They were asking how I know David, and I said I know him from school last year, but that didn't satisfy anybody. They all know him from school last year, and he didn't come visiting *them* at dismissal. I told them his mom was a friend of a friend, and Terry started in again, wanting names, until Natalie Brauer changed the subject. I don't think she did it to help me out. David is a touchy subject with her. When his name comes up, everybody looks her way. And she's the only one who hasn't asked me about him.

Natalie doesn't talk to me much anyway. She uses Mary as her go-between. Natalie's father is a doctor, and everybody loves her clothes and how she can have just about anything she wants. Her brother started at Princeton this year. So with me and Natalie, it's kind of like a world power sending an ambassador to talk with a third-world country. Natalie's pretty, too. If it weren't for that, I'm not sure she'd even be in this crowd. She's Jewish. But then, so is Ruth Fedderman. They're very close, but Ruth is much more down-to-earth, much friendlier to me. She's the one who actually invited me to come today. She said they were going to hang out at Mary's and that the others probably wouldn't mind if I came. Okay, so it wasn't exactly the warmest invitation, but it was the first time any of this crowd has brought me in on anything.

I said yes so quickly it made Ruth laugh. I wasn't the least bit cool about it. I even said "Wow" when she asked me. And Ruth goes, "I guess we'll see you later then."

Yolanda wasn't in school today. They took her mother to the airport. I'm glad she wasn't, 'cause I'm not really sure how I would have explained to her why I wanted to go to Mary's. I called home to tell Cait I was going to Mary Hennessy's house, which got Cait laughing.

"Are you teaching *her* how to read, too?" Cait said. Everybody knows Mary Hennessy is a pretty dim bulb. I told Cait to knock it off, but I could hear her telling Liam where I was going. "How many Hennessys does it take to change a light bulb?" Liam called into the receiver.

"How many?" Cait said, already laughing.

"Just one, once you show her which end screws in."

I had this dumb idea that we were going to do homework together. But in Mary's room we just looked at magazines and listened to Connie Francis, and they talked mostly about clothes when they weren't pumping me about David. It's all kind of boring really, except that it's so strange to be here that I've been excited the whole time. I like it better when they forget about me and talk about kids I know and things that have happened with teachers and stuff. They know way more than I do about people, like that Miss Cassidy had a miscarriage. I didn't even know she was married, which I was dumb enough to say out loud. "She's not," Ruth whispered. I've been trying to keep quiet ever since.

"She fell for this guy, and he left her high and dry," says Terry.

"It figures. She's kind of out of it," says Mary.

"That's for sure." Kathy laughs. Then she leans over to Mary and says, "Did you put it back?" I don't know what Kathy means but she sounds sort of serious, so I don't ask.

"No sweat," Mary says.

Mary has put the television on and she's skipping from channel to channel. Some of the channels are in color, and it's amazing to see. Mary's getting aggravated because President Kennedy is giving a press conference and a lot of the stations are carrying it instead of the soap operas. Nobody wants to watch it except Natalie. I do, too, but I don't say so. I like Kennedy. He's pretty handsome, at least for an old guy. On Mary's color TV, you can see that his hair is reddish, like in the pictures in *Life* magazine. But the thing I like best about him is how he says things that I'm afraid to say, like about Negroes. He actually went on television last June and told everybody to examine their conscience, and I watched my parents while they listened to him talk about all the wrongs that have been done to Negroes. He talked about equal rights and freedom, and even my mother was moved. She even thinks the Congress should pass President Kennedy's civil rights law, but if anybody dares to lift a placard to protest segregation, she calls them communist sympathizers—whoever *they* are.

"My father can't stand Kennedy," says Terry. "He never should have let the Negroes have that march in Washington." My father likes Kennedy even more than I do, but not for the same reasons. He likes him mostly because he's Irish. His brother Brian has a huge framed picture of him hanging in the firehouse where he works—right next to the Irish Republic's 1919 Declaration of Independence.

"The march just made everything worse," says Mary. "Now the Ku Klux Klan is bombing churches."

I've heard this logic before. It's the way my mother explains the bombing of the Baptist church in Birmingham, as if people demanding their rights is what killed those girls, not the hate. It's bad enough to listen to my mother spout this nonsense, but coming from kids my own age, it's really hard to take. I want to say something, tell them they've got it wrong. But they're so sure of themselves, and I'm only hanging by a thread here. I'm some kind of weird experiment for them, and if I say something like that, this whole adventure is over. So I don't say anything. I don't disagree or say what I really feel. I just sit here. I catch Ruth looking at me, wondering, I guess, if I'm going to say anything. She's seen me with Yolanda. They all have. That's when I see what's happening. They've triumphed and they know it. They know how I feel and why I'm not saying anything. I want to be one of them. They can give me what I want or take it away as they choose. Terry smiles at me, asks if I want another soda. They're leaving it up to me. Anytime I want to I can tell them that prejudice is wrong, that Negroes are human beings, too, just like us. That having Yolanda as my friend is no big deal. Anytime I want to I can say that and we can go back to the way things were on my first day back to school, when I was just *that weird girl whose family got evicted. Did you hear?*

So I'm not saying anything. Things have a chance to be different now. My folks are back together, and these girls are trying to be friendly. We don't have to agree on every little thing. They just think the same way nearly everyone thinks in this country. Nothing I say can change that.

15

How does everything get so complicated? All I did was accept their invitation to the Friday party at Natalie Brauer's tonight and already it's like a three-ring circus. I have to keep asking Brenda to repeat what she's saying about the jungle man and his search for turnips. My mind keeps drifting off, trying to figure out how I'm going to manage all this. Ambassador Hennessy reminded me three times today to be sure to ask David and his friends from the swim team at James Monroe High School to come tonight, too, like I didn't get the message loud and clear last night at Mary's, the first time they asked me to invite him. The last time Mary reminded me was after school, and Yolanda was already waiting for me outside.

Yolanda teased me all the way to her house about how the sorority sisters—that's what she calls Natalie's crowd— were being so friendly to me today. "What did you do? Give them your homework?" she said. I laughed and told her it was her fault. If she'd been in school yesterday, I could have avoided the whole thing.

But Yolanda's not really being fair. I mean Mary is no genius, but Natalie and Kathy are always on the honor roll and Ruth and Terry are decent students. I know they're not very friendly to Yolanda, but they don't single her out or anything. They're not friendly to any of the colored kids. But they just don't know Yolanda like I do. So now I have to ask David to come to the party, and that's about the last thing I want to do. He's going to think I like him or something. I mean, of course, I like him. He's a lot of fun, but I don't like him *that* way. And once I do that, he won't even want to be my friend anymore. He'll think I'm a pest.

Brenda wants to know what a eucalyptus tree looks like. I have no idea. She says we'll have to find a picture and put it in the margin. I don't know any magazines that have that many pictures of trees. Maybe *National Geographic*? Or maybe there's a *Bronx Tree Trimmers Monthly*? How will we know if we've found one anyway? I suggest a palm tree, but she won't go for it. I'm going to need help on this one.

There's only five minutes to go, but I don't see Cheryl getting ready to wrap up. I've still got to change for the party when I get home, talk Cait into letting me wear her green sweater. Brenda wants to know how come I don't know why they call October *October*. I walk her over to the dictionary on the shelf in the corner. "*Octo*—with a *c*—means 'eight' in Latin," I tell her, showing it to her on the page. We look at each other. It's not adding up. "If *octo* means 'eight,'" I say, more to myself than to Brenda, "how come it's the tenth month of the year?"

"Maybe the Latins can't count so good."

"Oh, you mean the Romans."

"The Romans?"

"Yeah. You know. Like the Roman Empire. *Spartacus.* Did you see that movie?"

She shakes her head no, wanting more information, but Cheryl is on her feet now and it's time to go.

"I'll see what I can find out about the eucalyptus, okay?" I say.

"Okay," Brenda says.

"And in the meantime, you're going to do your class-work like you promised, right?"

Brenda insists she will, but I'm not convinced. Cheryl said Brenda's teacher sent a note home about how Brenda has been restless in class again, falling even further behind in the work. In a way, it's really not her fault. School can be so boring. I hate it, too. But for some reason, I've never been the type to move a muscle without permission. I sit there like a robot, hoping nobody will notice me. But kids like Brenda are different. They're always reacting to the world, to the way things are. And when the world is boring—like school—they don't pretend that it isn't.

I help Brenda get her stuff together, then start folding the chairs. Yolanda comes over and takes a chair from me. "I'll take care of this," she says. "Mrs. Silverman is here. You don't want to keep her waiting."

"No. Right," I say, and Yolanda can sense I'm hiding something. I can see it in her face.

"You want to do something later?" she says.

I focus on getting my coat on. "Later?"

"Yeah. Maybe we could just go to Mr. Dixon's store and have an ice cream."

"I don't know. I'm supposed to go to Natalie's tonight."

"Natalie Brauer's?" she says, but there's no teasing in her voice now. She looks serious, a little shocked. I don't want Yolanda to be mad at me.

"Yeah," I shrug. "It's no big deal. I mean they've been trying to be friendly, so I figure it wouldn't really be right for me to say no." Yolanda doesn't say anything. "Anyway, I told my mother, I'd try to be friendly." That part's true. "I told her how mean they were my first day back, and she said maybe I wasn't being friendly." Yolanda gives me something like a nod and picks up the chair. Then she heads toward the front porch. "Are we still going to the park tomorrow?" I call after her.

"Sure," she says. "I'll see you tomorrow," her voice nearly swallowed by the porch.

Outside, Mrs. Silverman's station wagon is parked by the curb. Dusty is in the front seat, but David is waving me into the back with him. As I get in, the dog gives out a bark, as if signaling Mrs. Silverman it's okay to pull away. It startles me and David laughs.

"So how is the tutoring?" Mrs. Silverman says.

"I like it," I tell her. "I'm working with a third-grade girl."

"That's great," she says. "It's so good that you're willing to do this."

David rolls his eyes at his mom's comment. I'm not sure why. He doesn't seem to want to hear much of anything from his mom. He moves his gym bag so I'll have more room, but the car is so big, there's really no need. His hair is wet and I realize his mom probably just picked him up from swim practice. "How's school?" he says.

"It's okay. Better really."

"Better?"

"Well, the kids are starting to get a little friendlier."

"Good." He says it like he wants to know more.

"Some of the girls have been asking me to do things with them. You know. Just hang out." He nods, as if he'll take my word that this is a good thing. "In fact, tonight … they're … well …"

"What?" he says, seeing that I can't get it out.

I figure I might as well ask him and get it over with. "Well, there's a party at Natalie Brauer's." He doesn't exactly roll his eyes, but he has a funny look on his face. I say it anyway. "They wanted me to find out if you'd like to come over, maybe with some of the guys from the swim team."

"To Natalie's?" he says. He looks like he's about to laugh.

"Yeah," I say but so low he can hardly hear me.

"I'll pass," he says.

I don't know what to say, so I don't say anything.

"Sorry, Fiona. I just can't stand Natalie Brauer."

"David, that's very unkind," says Mrs. Silverman.

"Okay, Mom," he says, as if hoping to cut off any lecture

she may be ready to launch. "Sorry, Fiona," he says in a lower voice.

"It's okay," I tell him. "They just wanted me to ask you." I can tell he's embarrassed, and I wish I hadn't asked him. I could kick myself. We're quiet for what seems like so long, but it takes only a short while to get to Bryant Avenue. Mrs. Silverman pulls up in front of the house and says, "See you on Monday as planned?" I tell her yes. "Good," she says. "No, wait. Is that the eleventh?"

"I don't know," I say.

"David, isn't your swim meet on November 11."

"No, Mom. It's the twelfth."

"Good. Then I'll see you Monday, Fiona."

I say so long and open the door. David leans forward as I'm getting out. "So what's Yolanda up to, then?" He doesn't say "while you're with Natalie," but that's what he means. He knows she wouldn't be invited.

"She's fine," I say, pretending I don't know what he means. "We're going to the park tomorrow."

"In the morning?"

"Yeah."

"Maybe I'll see you there. I'll bring the hound."

"Okay," I say, and run upstairs, annoyed that I have to feel guilty for being invited to a party.

16

I hear Frank Sinatra coming from the kitchen, which means my mom's already started dinner. I don't want to eat though. I'm too excited.

Mom gets home about five from Dr. Kirshner's office on Tremont Avenue. She's his receptionist, but she takes care of his billing, too. The pay is awful, but he lets her go at four thirty, sometimes earlier.

"Hi, Mom," I say from the doorway. She nods. She's still in her high heels and has her jewelry on.

"Where's Cait?" I say, giving her a kiss on the cheek.

"Mrs. Kelly's," she says, and juts her chin toward the sink, where some string beans are in a colander, waiting to be rinsed off and cut up.

"Baby-sitting?" My mother nods. I hurry with the rinsing. "Do you think it would be all right if I borrow her green sweater?"

"I don't know, Fiona." She makes it sound like it would be a terrible risk.

"I'll be careful. Anyway, she gets all the new clothes. It's not fair."

"Oh, stop. That sweater was a birthday present from Aunt Helen."

"Yeah, and I still get games for mine. Can you talk to that woman?"

"I'll get right on it," she says with a laugh. "What's the occasion anyway?" She's got a suspicious look in her eye, like I'm hatching some plot to disgrace the family again.

"I got invited to Natalie's house."

"Natalie Brauer's?" My mother looks up from her potato peeling. She's impressed, or at least curious.

"Yeah, it's just a bunch of us hanging out."

"That's called a party."

"Well, I mean it's not an occasion or anything."

"There'll be no drinkin'. Is that clear?" She points the potato peeler at me like a blade. I give her my most offended look, and she puts the peeler down.

"So do you think it's all right?" I say.

"Of course it's all right. I'm glad to see you're making friends you can be proud of."

That's code for her opinion of Yolanda, but I don't say anything 'cause I don't want to hurt my chances for the sweater. I hate this. I hate feeling like she thinks I've suddenly joined her side, like I've changed my mind about Yolanda. I'll never change my mind about Yolanda. I just want the girls at school to like me. I want to have friends. I want to wear the stupid sweater. "Mom,

I mean the sweater. Is it all right if I wear the sweater?"

"I suppose there's no harm," she says. I bolt for the bedroom before she realizes there might be. "Dinner will be ready in half an hour."

"Half an hour?" I say, backtracking to the kitchen doorway. Since the potatoes aren't even in the water yet, I don't see how it will be. "Why so early?"

"Your father has the early shift again." She sounds almost glum. She likes it better when she doesn't have to see him in the evening, even if the late shift increases the chances that he'll go out drinking afterward like he used to.

"So where is he?" The early shift ends at three.

"He's getting some groceries on his way home," she says, but she doesn't look at me, and I know right away what scene this is. We're suspended, waiting to see when he'll get back. And when he does, how drunk will he be—just enough to tell a few Irish stories before dinner or enough to break up the furniture? Every minute past the time it should take to get groceries, we enter deeper into the dread zone, the place where you can't stop your brain from concocting reasons he might be delayed. And just when you've got yourself convinced he's fine, you remember what happened the last time you let yourself believe everything would be all right.

I don't want to do this anymore. I want to blot it all out, go to my room, and get ready for the party. I want us to be normal for once. But I can't leave my mother here to wait for him by herself. "So how was Dr. Kirshner's today?" I say.

But she doesn't want to do that, make small talk and

pretend things are normal. "Put those string beans into a pot, will you?" she says. "I need the colander to rinse off the potatoes."

This is the way she's been since we moved back. She goes through the motions, but she never pretends she thinks we're going to last as a family. It makes it a whole lot harder to believe we will. She doesn't talk about plans for us; she didn't even start delivery of the newspaper again. She's here because there's no other choice. And mostly I feel like it's my fault, like if I hadn't been getting into so much trouble—running away that day, and drinking wine at David's—she wouldn't have left Aunt Maggie's so soon. Maybe she could have saved enough to get us another place of our own. She doesn't mention what I did, but the guilt colors everything for me. If something happens, if she gets hurt again, it's going to be because of me. Why can't she just try to believe things can be different? I mean look at what happened to me. Who would have thought that Natalie Brauer and her friends would want me to do things with them? But it's happening. Yolanda says it all the time: if you act like a loser, that's what you'll be.

I take care of the string beans, without asking her any more questions. An Andy Williams song comes on the radio and makes me even more desperate to get out of the room. Mom lights the stove and puts a pot of water on for the potatoes. She stands next to me and tilts the colander, letting them plop in like a herd of clumsy divers. Before the last one makes it into the water, the apartment door opens. She hears it, too, because she takes a deep breath, steeling herself. Dad comes into the kitchen and puts the bag down on the table. "They had no pumpernickel," he says. He's sober. "The Germans got there first again." I laugh. My mother doesn't.

"Dinner won't take long," she says, and he comes around to stand behind us by the stove, almost touching.

"Smells good," he says, meaning the meatloaf, I guess. He leans over our shoulders, looking into the pots, and for a second I don't know if he'll stay or go. Then his body makes contact with my mom's, just a brush, accidental, and she flinches like a bee just landed. He feels it. We both do. And he steps back without a word, like the hunter who comes upon the fox with her leg in his trap. He heads back to the table, opens the bag, starts talking about Herb the baker, making like nothing happened, but Mom doesn't answer him. His shoulders are slouched, and I wonder how long it will be before he gives up. But he asks me about school while he clears the table, gets the dishes from the closet, keeps busy.

17

Terry Mazzarachio licks the pretzel for a long time before
she takes a bite. So I do the same. Little licks where your
tongue barely comes out of your mouth. None of the others
do much chewing either. I'm getting this. It's okay to hold
the pretzel between your lips for a spell, sort of like a twisted
lollypop, but chewing is definitely out. And they certainly
don't pull down as much soda as they can, then see who can
belch the loudest, the way Yolanda and I do. So I just hold
the glass as if I'm only vaguely interested in having any of
what's in it. I wasn't too far off on what to wear either. But
that's because I've seen them all on the avenue when they
go out. Capri pants. Matching sweater draped over the
shoulder. But I don't think I'm standing the right way, 'cause
they have a way of sticking their butts and their chests out at
the same time, and when I try it, I feel like I'm going to fall
on my face. And the hair thing is going to take me a while
to figure out. When they want to make a point, like about a
teacher they can't stand or a movie that was "dumb," they

make their hair swing off one shoulder and land around on the other, but when I try it, most of it lands in front of my face. I better wait until I can practice in front of a mirror.

The doorbell rings and Artie Brenner comes in with John Murphy. Then right after that Sal Matrone arrives with Tony Vincente—they all went to our school last year—and nobody stares at me or looks like they're wondering what I'm doing here. Natalie Brauer is being extra nice. She comes over to where I'm standing by the pretzel bowl and says little nicey-nice things, like what did I think of Mrs. Cornwallis's dreadful shoes today and do all the girls in my family have hair as red as mine. She doesn't stay long enough for the answers, but she's busy. It's her house and she's got a lot of soda to pour. I'm finding the pretzel-bowl zone a good position to play. You don't have to walk around to meet anyone, 'cause everybody finds their way to you at one point or another. The only problem is, I'm dying to chow down on the pretzels. I wouldn't even have to chew. I'd inhale them. That's how hungry I am. Dinner took an hour to get ready, and I had to leave half of it uneaten or I would have been late. I didn't realize—although I think this is what Liam was trying to tell me at dinner—that the later you arrive to a party, the cooler you probably are. I was early. In fact, Natalie looked at me so strangely when she answered the door that I thought I had the wrong night. She answered my hello, but her gaze went past me over my shoulder, then she leaned forward to look out on the front steps, as if someone might be out of view.

"Where's David?" she said. I didn't know what she was talking about, at least not right away. But instead of asking her what she meant, I said I didn't know. "Well, is he coming?" She sounded like she was holding something back—something nasty and angry—that she was sure to let loose if I gave the wrong answer.

So I said, "I think so," and she smiled as if I had wings on my back, which made me nervous, 'cause I knew David wasn't coming. "I mean he said he would if he could," I said. A look crossed her face, but I could see she wanted to dismiss whatever had triggered it. And she put her smile back on.

"Come on in," she trilled. "You're the first to arrive."

I didn't say anything, just handed her the giant-size bag of M&M's that my mother made me bring. She says you don't go to someone's house empty-handed. She's got a million of these Irish rules of order from the 1800s that she refuses to believe might not quite fit every occasion in the 1960s. Actually, what my mother wanted me to bring was the soda bread she'd frozen from last weekend, until Liam intervened for me. Natalie looked down at the bag in her hands like I'd given her my leftovers from lunch. She said thank you, like she was placating a crazy person, and offered to take my jacket.

"Can I help with anything?" I said. And from the way she looked at me, I wondered if I had fallen back on another of my mother's outdated rules without knowing it.

"Well, Rosa's in the kitchen," she said, and pointed the way. She headed for a closet. In the kitchen, I found Rosa. I thought Rosa was going to be a neighbor or something, a girl Natalie knew who wasn't from our school. But Rosa is the maid. It's incredible. She even wears a uniform. It's not black with a white apron, like a French maid's, but it's definitely a uniform. And Natalie's mother gives her instructions left and right. Even Natalie does. It's like you see in the movies.

My father says his aunt used to do wash for rich people when she first came over from the other side. She was young. She'd mend clothes, too. So I wonder if that's Rosa's story. Maybe she hasn't lived in New York very long. She looks Spanish. She didn't know what to make of my offer at first, but when she saw that I really wanted to help, it was fine with her, and she gave me bowls and things to take into the living room, where the party would be.

So far, helping Rosa has been the most interesting part of the night. I don't think I get yet what *party* means for these people. A party in my family means you eat a lot— chewing is uninhibited—and the music is loud and fast, and if you don't dance, they take your pulse to see if you're still alive. Toward the end of the party, the ones out cold from drinking are allowed to sit a few out. It's the same at my aunt Maggie's parties and at Grandma's parties. They've told me that not all families like to dance the way we do, but this crowd seems determined to block any urge, 'cause they keep putting on Bobby Vinton and Bobby Rydell and Little Peggy March. The best they could come up with was Lesley Gore before the boys got here and put on some Beach Boys. But by then, it was too late 'cause I was so hungry and nauseous from the music that I decided to sneak into the kitchen to chew in peace.

I found Terry in there, eating a banana. And we've been working on the rest of the fruit bowl ever since. Except now Rosa is making us sandwiches. When she came in and saw all the orange peels on the table, she insisted on making us something.

"I had to get out of there," Terry said when I came in. "I can't stand Tony Vincente."

I still haven't explained why I'm in the kitchen, although I think Terry has figured it out by now.

"You both like mustard?" Rosa says. She's about to top off two of the thickest roast beef sandwiches I've ever seen.

We both say yes, and in a moment the plates are in front of us and we dig in. I decide not to remind Terry that it's Friday and that technically, according to the Catholic Church, if we get hit by a truck on the way home, we'll go to hell just as fast as if we had made out with every boy at the party. Of course, the difference is the sandwiches are worth the pain.

"So you having a good time?" Terry says, her mouth full.

"Oh yes. Great time."

"Yeah, me neither. And the music rots."

I don't disagree, although I bet she means the Beach Boys, the only decent tunes we've heard all night.

"How'd you do on that math test today?" I say.

She shrugs her shoulders, seems uncomfortable. "Okay. How about you?"

"Not that great. I had number 3 right, and then I changed it. I don't know how Mary and the others do so well on all those tests."

"You don't?" she says, her voice low.

"No," I say, puzzled, but she doesn't tell me. Her eyes move toward Rosa putting away the meat, and I have to wait for my answer.

We talk about what a jerk Tony Vincente is until Rosa steps out of the kitchen. "Mary gets the answers," Terry whispers.

"To the tests? But how?"

"Well, somebody figured out, and I'm sure it wasn't Mary, that Cassidy brings her test in every Friday, complete with answers, and transfers the problems to a ditto sheet first thing in the morning. She runs the tests off in the office, but she leaves the sheet with all the answers under her blotter, and Mary has been taking the sheet from under the blotter."

"But how does she do it?"

"Nobody's in Cassidy's room first period, and Mary either gets a lavatory pass from Cornwallis or sneaks in between classes."

"But hasn't Cassidy noticed it's missing?"

"Mary returns it after third period. I guess Cassidy doesn't look for it until lunch, when she starts grading papers."

"But doesn't Cassidy think it's strange that Mary can barely keep up in class?"

"Well, Cassidy's mind's been on other things, if you know what I mean."

I remember what they said at Mary's house about Miss Cassidy having a miscarriage and figure it must be true after all. "Does Mary give the answers to anybody else?"

"Just Kathy, I think. I'm tempted to ask her for them, believe me, but it seems like a crappy thing to do. And besides, if my father ever found out, he'd go crazy. All he needs is one more thing to be pissed about."

I nod, wondering what her parents are really like, whether maybe she has secrets, too. But I don't ask. The sandwich is great and we concentrate on some full-tilt chewing.

"So what happened to David?"

I almost slip and say he didn't want to come, but I catch myself. "I guess he couldn't make it."

"You asked him, right?"

"Oh yes. Right away. He wanted to come. He just had some family stuff, and I guess he couldn't get away in time."

"Guess not," Terry says, although she's looking at me kind of funny. "I think Kathy's having something next week."

"She is?"

"Yeah, I'm sure you'll be invited. Maybe he can make it for that."

"I'm sure he'd have a great time," I say.

I don't know why that makes Terry grin, but she does.

18

It was the sound a head makes when someone gets smacked against the wall. I know that sound because I've heard it more than once. I'm not sure if that's what woke me. The house was really quiet when I opened my eyes. Maybe I dreamed the sound. My parents' room is right next door. But there's no reason to think there's anything wrong. Everything has been fine. Even Cait says so. Everything's fine.

It was only seven, too early to get up. And Yolanda wouldn't be at the park till nine. I wasn't sure when David would show. I rolled over on my side, facing the window. It was closed and I couldn't hear much of anything from outside. But I could hear voices, my parents' voices. They were whispering, but they were arguing. I couldn't hear what they were talking about, just a word here and there that got louder than it should. I reached for the book on the shelf above my head, a silly adventure thing that I got from my cousin Joe. I still haven't gotten things straightened out at the library yet. My record card is crossed out so many times with new addresses that they said I have to get a new card. But it takes a while. Change is upsetting for librarians, I guess.

I started reading—the lead character is stuck in the Yucatán, and he has lost all his gear (like who cares?)—and let the words blur me back to sleep. By the time I woke up for real, it was ten minutes to nine and I knew I was going to be late for Yolanda.

I didn't get to the park till about twenty after nine, and I've been waiting at least ten minutes. I don't see Yolanda anywhere, and this is where we said we'd meet, near the entrance. I look down the path that leads into the park, and I see someone a long ways down, walking toward the benches. It's Yolanda. I start after her, but I don't call her name. She's too far and I'd have to yell really loud. So for a minute or two it feels like I'm doing something sneaky, observing her while she's unaware.

She sits on the first bench, so she can watch the park entrance. She sits on the far end, maybe so she won't crowd the two women sitting at the other end. They notice her and stop their conversation. She gives them a wave, but they don't wave back. They just get up without a word. Yolanda turns away from them, faces the entrance. She spots me right away and waves. She doesn't see them sit down on the next bench. It's such an ugly thing to see—their moving away from her like that—that I can't believe it at first. I thought maybe it was a coincidence and the two were going for a stroll, but when they sat down on the next bench, I knew it was because Yolanda is colored. They might as well have turned water hoses on her. That's how hateful it is, but worse really because it's so petty. I want to do something, say something to get even with these women. But I'm a coward. It's easier to tell myself it's pointless to say anything.

Yolanda doesn't get up; she waits for me to reach her bench. And I'm wondering how annoyed she's going to be that I kept her waiting.

I sit down and she just says hi, waits for me to say something. "I'm sorry," I tell her. "Something woke me up really early, too early, and then I fell back to sleep and I overslept. I told my mother I wanted to get up early, but she must have forgotten."

"What woke you up?"

"I don't really know. I was just lying there remembering that I had heard something during the night, like something hitting the wall." I can't keep my voice from trembling.

"The wall of your room?"

"Yeah. I was just dreaming."

"What did it sound like?"

It's a simple question and I know the answer, but I feel like if I say it, say what the sound is, I'll start crying.

"What's the matter?" Yolanda says.

"Nothing," I tell her, because I don't want anything to be the matter. I know it was a dream, but if my mother's getting hit again, it's my fault, 'cause she never wanted to move back in with Dad. I know that.

Yolanda wants an answer. "What?" she says.

"Nothing. It was nothing."

"Fiona."

"It was ... it was like a thud, like when somebody's head hits the wall."

She doesn't get it. "Somebody's what?"

"Have you ever seen somebody get thrown against a wall?"

"No," she says, her voice small.

"My dad used to do that. And my mom's head would hit the wall. You'd swear it's going to crack open. It's such a horrible sound."

"Is he drinking again?"

"Oh no. Everything's fine."

"You sure?"

"Definitely. Even Cait says so."

Yolanda doesn't say anything. I glance over at the women on the next bench. They're staring at us. I want to give them the finger. "I don't know, Fiona. Maybe you better keep an eye on your mom."

"I do. We all do. Everything's okay." I wish she'd stop talking about it. "Have you seen David anywhere?"

"No. Did he say he was coming?"

"He said he'd probably be walking the dog."

"Let's go over by the field."

We get up and head in the direction of the women on the bench, who stare at us. "You take care now, ladies," Yolanda says to them as we pass, and her politeness does a better job than a finger ever could.

We walk toward the field, and our steps make noise in

the leaves. Yolanda still seems distant, not herself. She kicks at the leaves, digs her hands into her pockets. Finally, she says, "So how was it?"

I know what she means, but it takes me a second to get an answer out.

"The party," she says.

"It was fine," I say, but talking about it makes me feel almost as guilty as the thought of my mother getting hit again. I want to go to their parties; I want them to like me. But I don't feel right about it with Yolanda. They would never invite her under any circumstances. And that makes me feel like I'm wrong for going. But it's not fair. There are places all over the country where Negroes can't go—even universities. Does that mean I'd be wrong for going if I got accepted? "The music was pretty corny," I say.

"That figures."

"And snacking to them is sort of like farting in public. If you have to do it, keep it to yourself."

"That's because they all want to look like the skinny models in magazines."

"I guess."

"Sounds like a fun time."

I laugh, but I'm really happy to see Dusty, 'cause it's a perfect way to change the subject. She comes running at us, circling and sniffing, parking herself in front of us and giving us her paw. We both crouch down to pet her and soon David is beside us.

"Bad girl," David says.

"What did I do now?" Yolanda says, trying to make David laugh. She succeeds.

"She's not supposed to run away from me in the park. She knows that. But when she saw you two, she bolted."

"She looks like she knows what she's doing," says Yolanda.

"Have you guys been here long?" David says.

"Not really," I tell him. "I overslept."

"Oh, must have been a good party."

"It was okay."

"I'm sorry I couldn't go with you," he says, and Yolanda's expression changes. "I just can't stand Campbell and Brauer. And Hennessy … Jeez … if she knew how dumb she was, she wouldn't leave the house."

"Terry's nice," I offer. "And Brauer's not really that bad."

"Mazzarachio? Yeah, she's a good kid. But watch your back with Brauer." Dusty is leaping into mounds of leaves, digging for treasure. "Listen, I gotta head back. I have to help my dad with a bookshelf. Do you want Dusty to stay with you for a while? You could just drop her off on the way home."

"Sure," we both say at once.

"But I think you better put her back on her leash," I say. "I don't think she'll listen to us."

"Good idea." David calls Dusty over to him and snaps her chain back onto her collar. Yolanda takes hold of the leash and stumbles to keep up as Dusty pulls her. David says so long, and when Dusty realizes he's leaving, she stands still and starts to whine. "Stay," David tells her, and Yolanda comforts her, but it doesn't help. She keeps her eyes on him till he's long out of sight.

It doesn't take much to cheer her up though. We run with her and she loves it. When we tire out and land in front of a tree to rest, she parks herself between us, panting happily.

"Listen," I say. "It wasn't my idea to invite David to that party. They asked me to invite him."

"I figured that," she says. "Can I ask you a question?"

I knew this was coming. "What?"

"Why do you want to hang out with them anyway?"

"They're nice to me."

"Natalie'll be nice to anyone who can get her what she wants."

"What can I give her that she doesn't already have?"

"David."

"David?"

"Yup. She's got a thing for him. She followed him around like a puppy all last year."

"She's really pretty. I bet she could have any boy she wanted."

"Sure. Except she doesn't want them; she wants David, and he thinks she's ugly."

"She's not ugly," I say, and it comes out angry. Why does Yolanda have to make such a big deal out of this? So Natalie's a jerk sometimes. So what?

"Yes, she is. She's ugly on the inside."

"You're just feeling left out."

"Don't you worry about me. That's a group I like being left out of."

"What's so bad about Natalie? She's smart. She dresses great. She's interesting. She comes from a good family."

"And now you like it 'cause she's treating you like you matter, and then you can go around pretending you come from a good family, too."

If she had knocked me against the tree, it wouldn't have hurt as much. I feel weak. I get up, but I'm wobbly. Yolanda looks up at me. "I'm sorry," she says, but I have to get away. I need to be alone, where no one can see me, where it doesn't matter who I am or the kind of family I come from. I move away from her as quickly as I can, start walking toward the path.

"Fiona," Yolanda calls. "Fiona. Don't pay my big mouth any mind."

Dusty is barking, and Yolanda is calling my name, but I'm moving as fast as I can.

19

Liam has a job now at the A&P after school. He may really be straightening himself out. He's doing better in school. My mom makes him contribute five dollars from his pay toward the household bills, and she puts five dollars away for him. He's no saver. He'd spend every dime on records if he could. Tonight he came home with two: "Heat Wave" by Martha and the Vandellas and "Pride and Joy" by Marvin Gaye. They're great. Even my mother likes them.

When Liam put "Heat Wave" on for the sixth time, though, Mom chased us into his room. Dad's not home yet, and she's getting worried. It's way past time for me to go to bed, and I'll be tired tomorrow night because I'm going to Kathy's house for the Friday night hangout—they don't like to call it a party—but Liam and I got to talking. He always asks how Yolanda is. He doesn't say so, but he still feels bad about what happened to her. Yolanda says when Cheryl goes to his A&P, he bags for them and they always find extra stuff when they get home and unpack.

I tell him I had sort of a fight with Yolanda. When he says over what, I say "nothing really," and he tells me that's bullshit.

"She said something nasty, but she didn't mean it. Anyway, that's not what the fight was really about."

"So what was it about?"

"The girls I've started hanging out with."

"You mean Campbell and Hennessy and that crowd?"

"Yeah."

"So you don't hang out with Yolanda anymore?"

"Oh, I do. I mean we still do the tutoring."

"That's not exactly hanging out."

"I know, but it's hard."

"What's so hard about it?"

"We used to have lunch together, but now Terry Mazzarachio likes me to eat at her table."

"So why can't you bring Yolanda over with you?"

I look at him like he's got to be kidding.

"Too bad," he says.

"Anyway, Yolanda's been eating with Janet and Beverly."

"Colored girls?"

"Yeah. All this week, ever since we had the fight at the park on Saturday."

Liam stays quiet for a little while, then says, "This is really what you want?"

"What?"

"Well, to lose a good friend, for starters."

"Of course not. But Yolanda doesn't even try to understand."

"You mean she doesn't get why you want to be friends with a bunch of twits and princesses?"

"They are not twits."

"Well, what's Mary imitating, then?"

"Mary is fun. Anyway, not everybody has to be smart."

"Smart, no. But conscious is always a big help."

"That dumb stuff she does is mostly an act. She just does it to get attention. And she gets bad grades 'cause she doesn't want to do her work."

"So how is Hennessy a step up in the world for you?"

"She's not the only one in the crowd. There's Kathy Campbell and Natalie Brauer and . . ."

"Brauer. That's the Klansman's kid, right?"

"What are you talking about?"

"Dr. Brauer. They call him the Klansman."

"But they're Jewish. Why would he have anything to do with the Ku Klux Klan? The Klan hates Jews."

"I'm sure he's not in the Klan, but he's no John Brown either."

"What do you mean?"

"One of his patients asked him why he never had any Negro patients in his waiting room. And the answer he gave must have pissed her off, because she organized a miniboycott. It only amounted to about four patients, but he didn't like the word that was getting around. Bad for business."

"So what happened?"

"I'm not sure, but the stink ended. He probably went and hired some colored lady to sit in his waiting room twice a week."

"I never heard any of this."

"Mrs. Silverman's the one who started the whole thing."

"Mrs. Silverman started the boycott?"

"Yup."

"Oh, now I get it."

"Get what?"

"Why David wouldn't come with me to Natalie's house."

"You bet he wouldn't. But he never liked Natalie anyway."

I change the subject, get Liam talking about his boss at the A&P, but I feel really tired and tell him I better go to bed.

He says, "Thanks for attending the concert." I get up to go, but Liam whispers, "Wait. Listen."

I stay still. It's the front door. Dad's home. I start to open the bedroom door, but he stops me. I listen more closely. Dad is shuffling toward his room, mumbling something. I look at Liam. We don't have to say it. We know he's drunk. The disappointment surges up like acid in my throat. My eyes start to fill up.

"Didn't you know?" Liam says.

"Know what?"

"It started last week."

I sit back down. I don't want this. "Anybody can have a setback," I say.

"He hasn't been going to his AA meetings," Liam says.

"That doesn't mean he's giving up."

Liam lets out a sarcastic laugh. "Just don't get too comfortable here. We could be back at Aunt Maggie's in a week."

"I'm not going back," I tell him.

"What are we supposed to do? Stay here and let her go down for the count?"

"He'll get himself together. You'll see." Liam doesn't answer. I sit down to wait until we're sure Dad's gone to bed.

Liam puts on something by the Miracles, but he's got the sound so low I can barely hear it. He's singing to himself. He knows the words to every record he owns. That's how he gets through the waiting.

20

I wish I could remember the old saying my grandma uses for the expression that comes over a person's face when they're ticked off. It has something to do with the smell of cow manure. It would be just the right way to describe Natalie's face when I showed up at Kathy Campbell's house tonight without David. Nicey-nice went right out the window and in came the cold shoulder. I'm invisible again.

But David doesn't seem like a big issue for Kathy Campbell. She's still calling me flamethrower and asking me when she's going to meet Liam. And I'm not sure Terry Mazzarachio and Ruth Fedderman even remember I was supposed to bring David, because they haven't asked me about him. In fact, as soon as I got here, they dragged me into Kathy's bedroom to show me some bootleg cosmetics somebody was selling. Of course, I have no money, so I pretended not to like anything, which wasn't hard because the stuff was sort of weird—mostly glaring red lipsticks that went out with the '50s, right along with Rhonda Fleming, and gooey night creams that are sure to make your face break out. I did wish I could get the auburn mascara though. I've never seen that before.

Once the makeup was picked over, Terry and Ruth took me into the kitchen to show me the gun. It belongs to Kathy's dad. He's a cop and he keeps it on top of a cabinet when he's off duty, which is now, except he's sleeping. That's why we've been spared the Bobby Vinton songs, at least for another half hour or so, till he gets up for his shift. The gun is really big, and it's not silver like you see on TV; it's dark, dark gray, almost black. I touched the barrel with my finger, but it gave me the shivers. Nobody wants to ask Kathy if he's ever killed anyone. What a crappy feeling that must be, picking up your paycheck on Friday after you blew somebody away on Wednesday. Everybody deals with violence in his own way, I guess. At least a policeman is fighting crime. What's my dad fighting, besides us? What does he tell himself the next day when Mom's face looks the way it did this morning? I hate him so much sometimes, but never more than when I see the marks. I wish I could turn him in to Officer Campbell and let him get a taste of his own medicine.

Cait said she didn't hear anything last night and it's probably not what we think. She said Mom hasn't mentioned a word about going back to Aunt Maggie's. Cait's always right about this stuff. Mom usually talks about going to Aunt Maggie's after Dad gets like that. And she hasn't said a word.

"Ellen Traeger wants to be a policeman. Did you hear that?" Terry says.

"Yes, she wrote her vocation composition on that," I say. "But how many women policemen are there?"

"Probably seven in the whole country," says Terry.

"She just wants to hang out with guys all day," says Ruth.

"She thinks she's irresistible just 'cause Ron Oberman put his hand up her sweater last week."

"Whose sweater hasn't he been under?" says Ruth.

He hasn't been under any of mine, but I don't say so.

We get quiet when we hear the footsteps coming toward the kitchen, heavy, purposeful. It's Mr. Campbell. He's dressed in his uniform and Kathy's mother is with him, reminding him about something, although he doesn't seem to be listening. "Don't worry about it," he says to her. "I'll take care of it."

He greets us and wants to know why we aren't in there partying yet. Nobody knows what to say. "Well, don't let things get too rowdy, Mazzarachio," he says to Terry. She starts to laugh. "I don't want to have to get sent here on a domestic disturbance to quiet things down."

"That reminds me," says Mrs. Campbell. "Whatever happened with that call the other night, the couple on Daley Avenue?"

"The Randalls? She was beat up pretty good," he says softly, meaning for us not to hear.

"That must be the fifth time since the summer. At least the fourth."

"Well, she says she's pressing charges this time." He

reaches above the cabinet for his gun, and we watch him tuck it into his holster. The metal on leather makes a masculine sound, scary.

"Well, it's about time."

"She'll never go through with it. They never do." He looks into his lunch bag. "Throw another banana in there, will you? Mason's never got enough of his own." Mrs. Campbell adds another banana and an apple to the already bulging bag. "Anyway, that woman brings it on herself. She knows what he's like—and he's even worse when he drinks—but she stays with him, even gets him riled up."

"Yeah," Mrs. Campbell sighs, as if they've seen situations like this before and the Mrs. Randalls are always the real problem.

"Charges or not, if it happens again, a report has to go in. Child welfare authorities could step in and take the kids out."

"You mean they can take their children away?" I say.

"Don't you be worrying about that kind of stuff," says Mr. Campbell. "People like that bring on their own troubles."

No they don't, but I can't say that. Anyway, how do they know why Mrs. Randall stays with him? Maybe she has a daughter like me who runs away and sleeps on park benches and drinks wine till gases escape from her skull, and she feels like she has no choice, not to mention no money. Anyway, what's the right number of chances to give a person? It's not easy for some people to stop drinking. How do they know how hard it is for Mr. Randall? Dad says that everybody in AA has had setbacks. They tell you to expect them. So what is Mrs. Randall supposed to do in the meantime? Give up on him? Everything could turn out all right. You don't know.

Mr. Campbell kisses Kathy's mother good-bye, a brotherly kind of peck on the cheek, but I see the way his hand slides down along her side and I hear the little *tsk-tsk* she gives him and the smile. It's sweet, but it makes me think of my parents and I feel as homeless now as I was a month ago. Mr. Campbell says good-bye to us and already I can hear Bobby Vinton from the other room. Terry gets up to go into the living room, but I don't want to. It's not just the Bobby Vinton. I don't know what I want to do, except I feel like I should go home, make sure my mom's really all right.

Brenda didn't show up today. I should use the time to do my homework, but I can't settle down. My mind keeps dancing jigs. I can't get my father out of my head, can't stop thinking about what he's doing to my mom. I even wrote about it in my diary last night: "It's Sunday night, November 17, 1963, and it's the last time he's ever going to hit her." That's the truth. I'm going to put a stop to it. I don't know how yet. But I am.

I wind up in Yolanda's kitchen. There's always chocolate milk in the fridge, and Cheryl says I can have some anytime I want. So I take some milk and curl up on the big window seat that I never get the chance to sit on by myself, but the milk is giving me a stomachache and all I can see out the window is the rain blurring the view. The time is crawling by. It feels like Mrs. Silverman won't be here for hours.

I spot a magazine on the kitchen chair and take it back to the window seat. It's a copy of *Time* from September. The cover has a picture of George Wallace, that governor in Alabama, the one who stood on the steps of the university last June to block Negro students from registering. The story describes how President Kennedy had to send somebody from the Justice Department down to Alabama to tell the governor that if he didn't stand aside, he'd have to call in the National Guard. It's the kind of story that makes me feel good, makes me believe that you can put an end to things that are wrong. That's the way I felt listening to President Kennedy the night he delivered that speech on television about civil rights. That was the same day he stood up to Wallace, and he told the whole country that segregation and all the other stuff people do to Negroes was wrong, just plain wrong, and he's going to do something about it. We all have to do something about it. He makes me feel like we can really change things.

But in real life, in my life, it's not like that. It's almost impossible to change things. How can I make my mother stand up to my father, tell him he's wrong, instead of running away again? He's the one causing all the trouble. Except that when he's drunk, and even when we're just afraid he'll get drunk, it seems as if he's got all the power. All we think about is him. Like Friday night at Kathy's house. I mean it's not that I was having such a great time or anything, but I wound up going home just to see if my mom was all right. She was fine, but she was nervous as a cat all day Saturday. We all were. I don't know which makes me more upset—my father getting drunk and hurting everyone or the thought of having to move back in with my aunt again.

I hear the kids in the living room putting their books

away and folding up the chairs. I take the magazine in there and start helping.

Yolanda comes over to me. "Hi," she says. So I say hi. "You mad at me?"

The truth is, I am a little, but I've had so much on my mind since that day in the park that I haven't been thinking about it much. I shrug.

"You reading that?" She means the magazine.

"Yeah," I say. "It's got a story about the president and that governor. Pretty interesting."

"I read that one."

"Do you think Cheryl will let me borrow it? I didn't finish."

"She won't mind. Want to go out on the porch?"

I follow her outside. The rain has stopped, but you can still smell it. Yolanda hops up on the porch railing, sits in that same way I saw her that day after I slept on a park bench all night. All I wanted to do was get as far away from my dad as I could. And there she was, like she'd been waiting for me the whole time. That was more than a month ago. I still don't know what would have happened to me if it hadn't been for her.

"Listen," Yolanda says, "I'm really sorry for what I said last week."

I shrug. "It wasn't anything," I tell her.

"Yes it was. I'm sorry."

"Okay," I say. "It's okay." And it really is, 'cause I know she didn't mean to hurt me.

"You want to do something together?"

"Yeah, sure."

"Maybe Friday, after tutoring? We could go to a movie."

I don't want to make any plans for Friday, 'cause it seems like there's a good chance Terry's crowd will ask me to join them. "I don't think Friday would be good. How about Saturday?"

"Cheryl needs me to help her with something Saturday. Sounds like it's going to be an all-day thing. What's the matter with Friday? You'll be here for the tutoring anyway."

"I just ... I ..."

The expression on her face changes. She looks at me the way she does in school lately, when I'm with Terry or Ruth. "Forget it," she says.

"Yolanda, I want to do something with you. It's just that ..."

"It's okay. Forget it."

We don't say anything for a little bit. Then Yolanda says, "You worried about something?"

"I'm not sure yet."

"Not sure? A person is either worried or they're not."

I hesitate but only for a second. She's the only one I talk to about this. "It's hard to tell how things will turn out, but there are some bad signs with my dad."

"Drinking?"

"I didn't realize it at first, but Liam says he is."

"Jeez. That's bad."

"And Friday morning my mom looked like she ran into a wall or something."

"So, what are you going to do?"

"What *can* I do?"

"You say that about a lot of things."

"Well, there are some things I can't do much about."

"Your father is a bully," Yolanda says, and points her finger at the magazine in my hand. "If people didn't stand up to bullies, we wouldn't have a Negro student registered at the University of Alabama right now."

There she goes with her civil rights stuff again, so I don't say anything, 'cause she doesn't understand that this is different. My mom's not standing up to a racist; she's going to have to stand up to my father. And he isn't always a bad person. He really isn't. It's only when he's drunk.

"Of course, it took calling out the National Guard to get the job done," says Yolanda. Yeah, right, except George Wallace was breaking the law. The trouble is that not even Officer Campbell thinks what my dad does is against the law. And when my mom puts her foot down, she's not going to have an army behind her.

"Being a hero isn't always a smart move," I say, and hold the magazine out to her, as if to prove my point. "That guy Medgar Evers," I say, "the one who got shot the same night Kennedy talked on television—he'd probably be alive now if he'd been smart about it." I know this is going to get her mad, but I can't stand when she thinks she's got all the answers.

"You don't know anything about Medgar Evers," she says. She's off the railing now, in my face. "He stood up to the biggest bullies of all, the bullies in Mississippi. He stood up for us when hardly anybody had the courage to do it. He fought for our right to vote, our right to be a human being." Yolanda is breathless, her fists clenched. "He … he was one of the bravest men that ever lived. He was ready to die for what he believed."

"He got people mad. That's what happens when you try to change things. You get people mad."

"Well, *you* never have to worry about doing that, do you?"

"What do you mean by that?"

"Just what I said."

"Well, I don't get what you mean." Anger rises in my chest, like something backed up.

"You just go along with things. Things that are wrong. You don't even want to do anything about them."

"How do you know I'm not doing anything? Just 'cause I'm not getting beat up like all your heroes marching in Birmingham doesn't mean I'm not standing up for what's right." Yolanda's always going on about the people in CORE and SNCC who stand up to fire hoses and police dogs, but she's never done it herself. And she sure as hell has never been around anyone like my father, never had to watch him throw a Christmas tree across a room or put his fist through a wall.

"I haven't noticed you standing up for much of any-thing," she says.

"That's not true. How can you say something like that?"

"'Cause it's true. When things get hard, you don't want

to even look at them. You want to pretend they're out of your control."

"What are you talking about?" I say, but I know what she's talking about. She's talking about my not having lunch with her anymore and being willing to be around people who are mean to her sometimes, just so I can have friends. But she doesn't say that. She says something else instead, something even worse.

"I'm talking about how you left your brother that day, left him to get beat up."

"Yolanda, I told you how scared I—"

"And how you let your mother go back with your dad just so you wouldn't have to live with your cousins anymore. ..."

"But she—"

"... even though you knew what would happen. And now it's happening and you still want to pretend there's nothing you can do."

I stop trying to answer her because I know what I have to do. I have to get my own National Guard. I have to get someone who'll show my father what it feels like to be afraid. Anyway, this isn't really Yolanda talking. It can't be. I lean over the railing, stare out at the street. Yolanda starts crying. Something's badly wrong between us. So bad that I don't even have to ask her what's the matter. I thought I could be accepted by Natalie's friends without having to turn into someone else. But it doesn't work that way. I've broken the thing Yolanda and I had, the way we used to feel almost like the same person. Even now, I know exactly what Yolanda's feeling, and I know why she's crying. I feel like crying, too, because I don't want to lose her. But I can't stand up to Natalie and her friends for Yolanda. I can't go back to being the one nobody likes. I don't have that kind of courage. So I sit down on the step as if she isn't even there, and wait for Mrs. Silverman to come and separate us for real.

22

I guess Natalie has figured out that David isn't coming with me to anything they invite me to, because today the girls are getting together at Natalie's house and I'm not on the guest list. I figured it was all over after Friday anyway, when I showed up at Kathy's without David, but yesterday and today in school, Terry still wanted me to have lunch with them. And tomorrow, when they go shopping after school, Terry wants me to go, so I guess Natalie doesn't call all the shots. Tomorrow's Wednesday, and I'm supposed to be tutoring, but Yolanda won't even look at me. I'm not going.

I've got something important to take care of today after school, so it's just as well that I've been left out of Natalie's tea party. I'm going to the firehouse to see my uncle Brian, the oldest of my father's brothers. There are five brothers all together. When they were younger, they were in trouble all the time, always drinking and always fighting. There are bars in the Bronx they're still not allowed into, even though they haven't had a fistfight in more than ten years. Uncle

Brian is almost sixty now. Uncle Neil, the youngest, says they never started any fights, but they never lost any either. The trouble was, after a while they had such a reputation that guys would come in from Brooklyn and Queens to see what the big deal was all about.

One time a big Italian guy from Queens came into McFeeny's Bar with his two friends and walked up to my Uncle Liam and asked him if he knew where they could find some Irish guys called the O'Doherty brothers. Uncle Liam—he's about six foot three inches, looks like he wears football pads, and has hair as red as mine—told him, sorry, Luigi, the O'Doherty brothers all moved to Jersey City and there are no more Irish guys left in the Bronx. Everybody at the bar started laughing, and the Italian guy didn't like it much. Before long, the guy started swinging, but the problem was Uncle Liam was all by himself, so he had to take care of Luigi and his two friends on his own, at least until my uncle Brian got there, and that wasn't until Uncle Liam was hurtin' pretty bad. That was the beginning of the end, Uncle Liam says. It was starting to affect his looks. It was also affecting his marriage. Aunt Mary said if he got into one more fight, he could go join the world wrestling tour, because she wasn't letting him back in the house.

My uncle Brian is washing the truck. They wash the truck a lot at this firehouse. My mother says it's 'cause Uncle Brian doesn't drink anymore and he doesn't want to sit around with nothing to do. He and my father haven't exactly been talking for a long while. I'm not really sure why. When my dad stopped drinking after the eviction, I thought that might get them back together, but it didn't.

"Well, look at you," he says, and I know it's because he hasn't seen me in two years, since my confirmation. And I guess I've changed. "You'll be as tall as your brother soon." I smile, mostly because he's smiling so big that I can't help but do the same. "Come sit down," he says, pointing to the bench along the driveway. I sit down. He sits down next to me, and I don't know how to even start this.

"So," he says, "I don't suppose you came here to help wash the truck."

I shake my head. He's all gray now, no red in his hair at all. And his face looks older than I remember, too old. Maybe he's too old to help me with this. My image of him is all confused with the stories people have told me; he just looks like an old man, an old man who can't do much about anything. I shouldn't even bother asking him to help me with my dad. "Terence is going to Fordham, started this year," he says. I can tell he's proud of this. "Be good if he makes something of himself, not like us." He means himself and his brothers.

I like Terence. He's really handsome and a great singer. At family parties, when we would come to the part where everybody takes turns singing, Terence and his older brother Joe always sang "Four Green Fields," and Grandma cried every time. Joe drinks heavy now. My mom says it's bad. I ask Uncle Brian how Kathleen is, and he says she might get married. But he shakes his head as if he doesn't like the idea, and I wonder if she's marrying Tony, the guy she's been seeing since she was in high school. He's Italian. Kathleen used to baby-sit for us. We loved it. She's only four years older than Liam, and we used to stay up late, even feed the cats chocolate. I really miss my cousins. I don't ask who Kathleen's marrying. I'm not in the mood for another O'Doherty lecture about the evils of ethnic mixing.

"Is everything all right?" he says. I tell him yes, too quickly. He doesn't look as if he believes it. He puts his hand lightly on my knee. "I know things haven't been so good," he says. "But your father's going to AA meetings now. Things will change."

"Uncle Brian."

He looks at me, seeming not to want me to say anything, then he looks away.

"Nothing has changed."

He sighs, folds his arms across his chest. "It takes time," he says, as if I'm some impatient little kid waiting for cookies to finish in the oven.

"You don't understand," I tell him. And I wish he wouldn't make me say it. His eyes squint, like he's suspicious, like I'm someone who can't be trusted to keep silent about things that shouldn't be said out loud. "He's still doing it, still hitting her."

He flinches. But I'm determined to say what I came here to say. "I need your help."

"There's nothing anybody can do about these things, Fiona."

"Yes, there is."

"Fiona." He's exasperated now.

"If he tries it again, if he hurts her again, I want to know I can call you."

"Fiona, I can't be interfering in a thing like this—"

"Yes, you can."

"It's not my business to be—"

"When you were younger and your brothers were fighting, getting beat up, didn't you step in and help them? Didn't you do everything you could—even risk getting hurt yourself—to stop it?"

"That was different."

"Yes, it was different. They were grown men. And they could defend themselves. This is my mother. And she can't. I don't want to wake up in the morning anymore to find her eyes black or her lip swollen. All I'm asking is, if it happens again, that you come over and help me stop it."

"Fiona, this is between your mom and dad. It's not my business to be interfering—"

"Whose business is it, then? The police? Should I call the police next time?"

"That's the worst thing you could do."

I know he's right. I think of what Kathy Campbell's father said about how that woman's children might be taken away by the authorities if there's one more police report about her husband beating her up. "Then who's going to help me?"

"Oh, Fiona," he says, like I couldn't possibly understand what this is about. But that's all he says for a long while.

So finally I get up, 'cause I'm pretty angry and I don't want to look at him anymore. And whatever his reason is for not helping me, I don't want to hear it. And I never want to hear another story about how well Brian O'Doherty and his brothers could stand up for themselves, because they don't stand for anything. And that's what I tell him. I head back down the block from where I came. I've got more than fifteen blocks to walk, but I don't think about how far it is, I just go, tracing the cracks in the sidewalk ahead of me. I must be four blocks away from the firehouse before I hear his steps pounding hard behind me. I stop and turn, and he stops, comes only close enough for me to hear him. "If I'm not home, dial the firehouse," he calls to me. "They'll know where I am."

A man leaning on a parking meter, curious, looks toward my uncle all red in the face, then at me. The man doesn't understand what this means to me. To him it's just a curious exchange, made even stranger when I run to my uncle and hug him so hard we fall against a storefront.

23

I got my uncle's home number from my mother's address book. I had to look up the firehouse number in the phone book. I wrote them on the inside of my wrist so there's no chance I'll lose them, and they make me think of concentration-camp survivors. I retrace the numbers every few hours. I have them memorized already, but I'm afraid that if I get nervous or scared, I might forget them.

I guess if Yolanda knew I went to talk to my uncle yesterday, she'd think it was because of what she said to me, because of how ashamed I am of the coward I've been. And she'd be right, but only partly right. Thursday night, in Liam's room, when he said the drinking had already started, I made up my mind I was going to do something about it this time. And I am. 'Cause now I have my own army to call on, like Kennedy had in Alabama. Yolanda says I act as if I have no choices at all. And the way things are now, maybe I don't. So I'm going to change the way things are. I've got a plan.

Yolanda came over to me twice already today. She looked

pretty upset, but I'm not ready to talk to her yet, not until I've finished what I'm going to do the next time my father goes out drinking. Then I'll be able to tell her. And she won't have to look at me that way anymore, like I'm someone she can't respect.

Terry and Ruth and the rest of the crowd were supposed to go shopping on the avenue after school, but it was raining, so Terry invited everybody to her house. Terry's mother is really friendly, and she's been feeding us ever since we walked in. She made us hot chocolate to have with the Italian cookies from the bakery; now she wants us to have ice cream. Natalie's still not talking to me, but everybody else is. Ruth even asked me why I didn't go to tutoring. I said they canceled it today, which isn't true, but I didn't want to talk to her about Yolanda. Still, I feel bad about not going to tutoring. I know I'm letting Cheryl and Brenda down.

"What's the matter?" Terry says.

"What?" I say. We're all squeezed into her bedroom, all of us except Natalie and Kathy, who are somewhere else talking. I didn't even realize Terry sat down next to me on the floor.

"You look like you're somewhere else."

"Oh, I'm fine. Sorry." Terry wants to show me something in *Seventeen*. It's an article about the invention of contact lenses. You wear these little round plastic things right on your eyes instead of glasses and you can see clear as a bell. Terry would give anything to have them. She hates her glasses. I can't blame her. They're pretty thick. Ruth turns on the television and finds *General Hospital*. She says she hates to miss it. Mary says Ruth is addicted. She might be. But still, it's kind of nice sitting here watching it, on a TV in your own room, with all your friends. It feels good to just hang out, not to have to worry about anything.

It's not like this at my house, that's for sure. And the magazines you see around Yolanda's house are mostly serious ones like *Time*. The stories give you plenty of things to worry about. Yolanda showed me a story they did in August on this guy named Roy Wilkins. His picture was on the cover. He's an old colored guy, head of the NAACP, stands for the "advancement of colored people" or something. It's another one of those civil rights groups Yolanda and her aunt are always talking about. But Yolanda wanted me to see the story so I'd understand how hard things really are for colored people. One part talked about how they can't get jobs or get into colleges. They can't even register to vote. President Kennedy is trying to fix all that. He wants to pass a law to change a lot of this stuff. Even my parents say there should be a law against some of these things, like segregation especially and not being allowed to go to school. But I'm not so sure they'd agree if it wasn't for President Kennedy. That's why I like him so much. He helps people see when things are wrong. And he's trying to do something about it.

Maybe I could write to him and ask him to talk sense to my father; he's the one person my father might listen to. That's what I envy most about these girls. They have no worries. The grown-ups do all the worrying for them. They don't have to figure out how to keep their dad from drinking or keep their mom from taking them to another part of the country. They just have to figure out what to wear and maybe do the dishes once in a while. The biggest problem they have is when some boy they're crazy about isn't crazy about them. But they wind up talking so much about it that there is no time left to feel anything anyway.

Right now I wish I wasn't feeling anything either. I wish *General Hospital* could keep me from feeling so bad about not tutoring Brenda or missing Yolanda or worrying about my dad.

24

Sometimes the bartender at Gerrity's takes my father's keys away from him, and he has to walk home. When they make him leave, he goes to the Knights of Columbus Hall and drinks there. I'm sure that's where he is now. To get home, he'll have to pass this corner. And he'll have to pass me. It's dark and a little cold. So I've been stepping inside the drugstore now and then, hanging out in the phone booth just inside the door. The lady behind the counter has been looking at me sort of annoyed, but I pretend I'm talking on the phone. I can see the street through the front door, even from the phone booth, so I know he hasn't passed. He'll be staggering for sure by now.

I hung out at Terry's again tonight, didn't get home till almost nine thirty. The house was totally quiet, so I knew something was up. The lights were out and I stumbled over the leg of an end table, broken and lying in the middle of the room. Pieces of broken glass from the Tiffany lamp were picking up street light from the window and reflecting it back in night colors. It looked like modern art, like it had no meaning.

My mother was in her bedroom. She had a suitcase open on the bed, but she was mostly just staring at it. The only light she had on was the little night-light she keeps near her statue of the Virgin Mary. "Mom," I said. She didn't look at me. I came closer to her.

"Get ready," she said. It was a whisper. "We're going to Aunt Maggie's."

I sat down near her on the bed. Even in the dim light, I could see the cut at the top of her cheekbone, near her eye. It didn't seem to be bleeding anymore, but it was bad.

"Is Aunt Maggie going to take you to the hospital?"

"I don't need a hospital," she said, her voice hoarse, as if she'd been crying hard. She had a shirt in her hands and started folding it.

"I think you should let a doctor look at that."

"Go, get ready," she said.

I stood next to her for a moment. Was she getting shorter? I put my arms around her, hugged her, although I didn't expect one back. In the kitchen Liam and Cait were sitting with Owen. Cait's face was all red. Liam was staring out the window, stone-faced. "Don't let her go anywhere until I get back," I said to Cait.

"What do you mean 'get back'? Where are you going?"

"Don't let her go anywhere. Don't any of you go any-where," I said. I left the apartment and headed straight for Gerrity's. I went the way Dad always goes, so I'd see him if he was heading back home. He didn't pass me. His car was on the side street near the tavern, but I was betting he wouldn't be in the tavern anymore. The place was crowded for a Thursday night. The noise was a mix of glasses bumping into glasses, words into words. I headed straight for the place where the bar turns a corner, the place where the bartender hangs his towel. I waited there till he noticed me. A few of the men at the bar greeted me, but they didn't say much. They knew why I was there.

"Fiona," Mr. Corrigan said when he saw me. He's the bartender. I've known him all my life.

"I've come for the keys," I said.

"He got home all right?"

"He got home," I said. The rest was our own business.

He reached under the bar, took only a second to find them, and handed them across to me. I thanked him and turned away. "Wait," he said. "Let me give you a Coke."

"No, thank you," I told him.

When I got to the drugstore, I bought myself a *Daily News* and a Hershey bar, and I've been eating pieces of it real slowly. There's a bench two doors away. That's where I eat the chocolate.

There's a picture of President Kennedy and Jackie on the inside page of the newspaper. He's down in Texas and he made a speech today, Thursday, November 21, talking about his hopes for the space program. It's really a dull story, about what a challenge it's going to be, but further on there's a great quote from the president. It's about the writer Frank O'Connor and how as a boy, when he and his friends came to a wall they thought they'd never be able to climb, they'd throw their caps over. That way they had no other choice but to follow them over. Seems to me like that's how President Kennedy decided to do something about the way colored people are treated. He knew a lot of people were not going to want to hear about it. Cheryl says that for a long while he didn't want to get voters annoyed at him. But he started talking about it anyway, and now the whole country has to do something about it whether they want to or not—and he does, too. That's the way I feel right now. What I'm doing about my father is something I thought I never could have done. But now my cap is over the wall, and I've got to follow. That's the way Yolanda does things. She doesn't wait so long that she's paralyzed by fear. She does what she needs to do.

It's getting late now. It's almost eleven. But I had a big dinner at Terry's house, so I'm not really that hungry. The drugstore is closing, and I'm worried that I may have missed him somehow. Maybe I should go home and see if he's there.

I start walking toward the apartment. It's only a few blocks. I don't understand how I could have missed him. I feel the keys in the pocket of my jacket; they slap against my thigh as I walk. I can't get the words to a stupid song by Bobby Vinton out of my head—"Blue on Blue," the one Terry was playing at her house—so I start humming "Don't Make Me Over" by Dionne Warwick. There aren't many people on the street, and when I turn down 174th Street, I see Liam sitting on the stoop.

He stands up when he sees me. "Where have you been?" he calls. I shrug. "You better get over to Aunt Maggie's."

"Is that where they are?" He nods. "Where are you going to stay?"

"I don't know," he says. "Probably at Kevin's." I don't tell him what I'm planning to do. "I better walk you to the bus stop," he says, but I tell him I'll be okay.

"I need something from upstairs. Is he asleep?" I ask.

"Out cold. He wouldn't touch you anyway."

I hope that hasn't changed.

Liam heads down the block, but not toward Kevin's, and I go upstairs. The living room is as it was, but the glass is picked up. Most of the dinner dishes are still in the sink. He must have come back home before they could finish cleaning up. I go into my room, get undressed, and set the alarm for six o'clock. I take the house keys off the ring and hide them in one of the black shoes Cait used to wear on Sunday, the ones that will be mine once they fit me.

I awoke before the alarm, so I washed the dishes and cleared the table. I'm sitting on the couch in the living room, waiting for my dad to wake up. My schoolbag is by my feet. I'm going to school, just like any other day, and I'm going to see all my friends, just like any other day.

He's awake now, but he doesn't know I'm here. I hear the toilet flush, and I hear his footsteps crossing the kitchen toward the living room. I have everything memorized.

He stands in the doorway and says my name, startled. "Where is everyone?" he says.

"They're at Aunt Maggie's."

He shuffles in, moves toward the window. "Guess that's best," he says.

I can barely look at him. He thinks he can stand here and act like some weary old soldier, returning to the battlefield—after all the mess and the wounded have been nicely cleared away for him.

"No, that's not what's best," I say. This isn't one of the

things I've practiced to say, but it's as good a way to start as any.

"What?" he says. "Did you say something?" He looks so tired, sickly really. His shirt is open over his pants and he has no shoes on.

"I said that's not what's best."

He doesn't answer me, doesn't understand, probably doesn't even think what I say is anything he needs to listen to.

"What's best is for you to leave."

"What are you talking about?"

"You're the problem, not us. You need to leave."

He makes some kind of sigh and looks back out the window. He's going to ignore me, act like his headache and his remorse are all he needs to tend to.

"Here are your keys," I say in a voice I know he can hear.

He turns and looks at me, but not at the keys. "What's gotten into you?" he says. He sounds annoyed now.

"You're the problem," I say again, "not us."

He looks at the keys now, sees that the house keys are gone. "What did you do with my house keys?" he says.

"You don't need the house keys. You don't live here anymore." He stares at me, but I can't read his face. I don't care what he thinks about this anyway. I just want him to go. "I'm not moving back with Aunt Maggie. Neither is Mom or any of us. You need to go find a place to live."

"What are you talking about?"

"I'm talking about you. You're the problem. We shouldn't be the ones who have to leave."

"I haven't asked anyone to leave. They can come back anytime they want."

I hear myself laugh. I don't mean to. It just comes out. He drives everyone away and doesn't even see it.

"They are coming back. But you're going to be gone. And if you come back here again, I'm calling Uncle Brian."

"You can call anyone you like," he says, angry now. "Call the whole family."

I stand up. "I'm calling Uncle Brian and he's going to help you move out."

"He's not going to help anyone. He hasn't even seen any of us in two years."

"He's seen me. I've talked to him. I have his word that he'll help us if you ever come back here."

He stares at me, lost. "And what's he going to do about it?"

"What you do to Mom."

"Give me my keys," he says, taking a step toward me.

I walk over to the phone, pick up the receiver, dial Aunt Maggie's house.

"What are you doing?" he says.

"Calling Aunt Maggie so you can talk to Mom."

He stares at me, dumbfounded, while I dial. Uncle Eddie answers and I tell him that Dad wants to talk to Mom. Uncle Eddie tells me everyone's worried about me, but I tell him I'm fine. I hear him talking to someone else. Then he tells me my mother won't come to the phone. She doesn't want to talk to my father. "Then Dad would like to give you a message to give to Mom, okay?" Uncle Eddie waits on the line, and I hold the receiver out to my father. He stands there, stunned. "Tell Uncle Ed you're leaving here and never coming back and that Mom can come back home." My voice is trembling.

Dad looks at me, finally seeing something. "What happened last night?" he says. "Is she hurt bad or something?"

"She'll be fine," I tell him, "once you're gone." He looks down, as if he's sad or hurt, but I don't believe that anymore. "Tell him," I say, and he comes to the phone.

"Fiona, I'm sorry. It's the drink that does this."

"I don't care what it is, and I don't care if you're sorry." He looks at me as if something has fallen into place, something he's been expecting somehow for a very long time.

He takes the receiver, clears his throat. "Eddie?" he says. "Tell Bridget … tell Bridget she can come home. I'm going to find a place to stay till I get straightened out. I won't be bothering her." Uncle Eddie asks him something and my father answers yes.

I put on my coat and pick up my schoolbag. I walk to the door, open it. The light coming in from the window colors the pieces of glass that someone has put into the wastebasket. When I hear Dad hang up the phone, I close the door behind me.

Outside it's cold and I close my coat. A few doors down I catch my reflection in the hardware-store window. My hair is wild and curly, and I realize I forgot to comb it. But I don't care. I like the way I look today.

It's weird the things that play in your head some days. Today it started on the way to school, a jingle from a toothpaste commercial. It's stupid, but it's better than thinking about what happened this morning and whether my mother will come back home or not. "You'll wonder where the yellow went when you brush your teeth with Pepsodent." It's so disgusting to imagine someone having yellow teeth, but it's such a happy tune—the kind you could skip down the block to—that you'd swear yellow teeth were as common as bad breath. The tune's been slipping in and out of my head all morning. In first period, I was glad when Cornwallis gave us a reading assignment, 'cause it helped crowd it out. But in its place came thoughts of my father and what might happen tonight. I read the story as fast as I could, hoping it would keep my mind off home.

It didn't. I could barely concentrate on the page. Ten minutes into the assignment, Mary Hennessy asked for the lavatory pass. She was off to get Miss Cassidy's test. I've paid more attention to this routine ever since Terry told me about the cheating. It's surprising that Cornwallis hasn't caught on, but maybe because it happens only once a week, the pattern isn't that easy to spot.

At lunch, Terry's constant talking was annoying me. She kept asking me what was wrong, which I couldn't tell her in a million years. So I went and sat by myself, told her I had to study for the math test, which I did, but really I was hoping Yolanda would come over. She didn't. She tucked her schoolbag by the wall and went outside to play kickball. I followed her outside just to see what she was up to, but I mostly watched Mary and Kathy and Natalie having this intense talk. Midway through it, the three of them practically ran back into the lunchroom.

Lunch is over now and I'm in Cassidy's classroom. She looks awfully angry. Something's wrong. She's standing at her desk with her arms folded and staring at the last of the kids walking in. Everybody is quieter than usual. We wait. "We're not having a test today," she says. There's a sigh in the room, but only halfhearted, 'cause everybody can see there's more to the story. I look at Mary. Her face is a little flushed, but otherwise she's calm. "We're not having our test today because my answer sheet is missing from my desk." That explains it. That must be what the schoolyard summit meeting was about: Mary didn't get the answer sheet back in time. "No one is leaving this room until I find it. Open your schoolbags."

There's silence for a second, then the air fills with the

sound of zippers like a swarm of overweight bees. I look at Mary. She doesn't even hesitate. She's got her bag wide open. Miss Cassidy walks between the first two rows, looking inside the bags but not touching anyone's things. She turns up the row between me and Yolanda, who sits across from me. I can't see Yolanda's face because Cassidy is standing between us now, so I can't see her reaction when Cassidy says, "Can you explain this?"

A couple of small gasps and mumbles bubble up, but the class is mostly quiet. I lean back so I can see Yolanda. She's staring straight ahead. Miss Cassidy has something in her hand now, a paper. I realize it must be the answer sheet that Mary always steals. "Answer me, Yolanda," Miss Cassidy says. "Can you explain how you have this in your bag?" Yolanda won't look at her. She's staring straight ahead, into nothing. Miss Cassidy's hand is trembling, the paper vibrating as if caught in a current of air. She waits for an answer, but Yolanda won't talk. She's sitting up straight as an arrow, her mouth tightly shut.

Miss Cassidy walks to the front of the room with the paper in her hand. She stands in front of the class, looking extremely upset, as if she's going to cry. "Does anyone else know anything about this?" she says.

No one says a word. I look over at Mary and Kathy. Mary is busy twirling a lock of hair, seeming bored with the whole business. Kathy glances at Yolanda with a contemptuous look, as if her suspicions about her were now confirmed. I remember how intensely Mary and Kathy were

talking during lunch, how they ran back into the lunchroom, where the schoolbags were. Yolanda's is easy to spot.
She keeps her scarf tied to it, the purple one, her favorite. I
know what they did. They put the answer sheet in Yolanda's
schoolbag.

Still, no one has answered Miss Cassidy's question, so
she goes to her desk and reaches for her referral pad. When
she's about to send someone to the principal's office for dis-
cipline, this is what she does, goes right for the pad—no
warning, no lecture.

I don't recognize my own voice when it comes. It's clear
but weak. "Miss Cassidy?" I say.

She looks up, and I'm stunned for a second, frozen.
"Yes," Miss Cassidy says, her hand still poised over the pad.

I can't speak. She waits, but I have no voice. Mary and
Kathy are looking at me. So is Terry. It will all be over if I
say anything now; they'll never speak to me again. I'll be
an outsider for good. I look at Terry. I think of how hard it
is to walk into the cafeteria when you know that no one is
waiting for you, that no one wants you at their table. There's
nowhere to look when you eat by yourself, no one to be,
nothing to take your mind off what waits at home.

Miss Cassidy starts writing again, and so I know it's
time.

"Miss Cassidy," I say, "Yolanda didn't take your answer
sheet."

Cassidy looks at me. "Did you take it, Fiona?" she says
softly.

I shake my head no. Seconds pass. People start whispering.

"Fiona?" Miss Cassidy says. She's losing patience.

"May I talk to you outside?"

The silence splinters then, into countless private exclamations. The room is thick with expectation, eyes shifting from Mary to me to Yolanda. Miss Cassidy tells me to come with her, and I follow her to the door without a word, but by the time I reach it, no one's bothering to whisper anymore, and I can hear my name and Yolanda's and Miss Cassidy's rising in the room like whitecaps in a storm.

Outside, Miss Cassidy and I walk across to the other side of the hall. We can see into the principal's office from here. The door is open. "Tell me what you know," she says to me. "This is important."

"Someone in the class has been taking the answer sheet from your desk during first period since the beginning of the year. She puts it back before class starts."

"Fiona, are you saying you know …," she says, but she's distracted. We both are. There's a sound coming from the principal's office, the sound of someone crying. We move toward the sound, wondering what's wrong. It's Mrs. Reynolds, the school secretary. She's crying and so is Mrs. McVeigh, the assistant principal. Miss Cassidy goes to the doorway. "What's wrong?" she says, sounding as puzzled as I am.

"President … President Kennedy was shot," Mrs. Bergman says. She's our principal, but I've never seen her look so serious, so sad. "The radio is saying he's dead."

Miss Cassidy grips my arm tightly, as if I might fall if she doesn't hold on to me, or *she* might. "Oh no," I hear her say. "Oh no." And she starts to cry. All of the grown-ups are crying now, even Mrs. Bergman. Miss Cassidy steps into the office, then out again, seeming at a loss for what to do. "Should we tell the children?" she says.

Mrs. Bergman wipes her nose with a starched hankie, the kind with the pink stitching that is always peeking out of her jacket pocket. "I'll tell them," she says. "I'll visit each classroom separately."

Miss Cassidy leads me back toward the classroom. "We'll talk about the test another time," she says. She's still crying. I am, too, although I'm not even sure why. The day has been slamming me against a pier like a piece of driftwood.

When Miss Cassidy tells the class that Mrs. Bergman will be coming in to talk with us, I'm sure they all think it's about the test. Miss Cassidy tells us to sit quietly and read a book.

"You mean our math book?" David Pincus asks her. Questions like these are why the kids call David pinhead. But Cassidy is too upset to answer. She just sits at her desk, waiting for Mrs. Bergman to come and tell us what has happened.

The shock spread like a poison gas, the awfulness of knowing that something you thought was too terrible to happen can really happen. A lot of the kids were crying. The teachers talked in small groups. They didn't ring the bells for the last two classes. We were allowed to go to the auditorium or the cafeteria if we wanted. I chose the cafeteria. I don't know where Yolanda is. She didn't come with me after Cassidy's class, didn't even look at me. I'm writing a letter to Terry, but it's hard to do. I feel bad about what I did. I've never told on anybody before in my life. And now, in the space of three days, I've told Uncle Brian about my father and come an inch away from getting Mary into what's sure to be a whole lot of trouble. How can I explain that I had no choice? How could I ever look at Yolanda again if I let them do that to her? Yolanda might never know that I could have rescued her. But I would know. I'd know that I was an even worse coward than she thought.

When the dismissal bell rings, nobody rushes to the doors

the way they always do. It's as if there's a thick fog to get through. My fog is filled with thoughts of my mom and whether she'll be home. People in the streets are gathering in little groups in front of stores, on stoops, sometimes in the middle of the street. The TVs are on in the window of the appliance store, and people are gathered there, watching the screens, wiping their eyes. I peek through and see Walter Cronkite, looking serious and sad. I can't hear what he's saying. I can't help wondering if the civil rights bill President Kennedy wanted to pass will ever have a chance now, but I push that thought away. I move on, and up ahead I see someone leaning on a car outside my building half a block away. It's Yolanda. She comes toward me, all her armor melted, her attitude gone. She seems softer. "Can I talk to you?" she says when I'm only a little bit away.

"Sure," I say.

"You didn't have to do that," she says. The sun is in her eyes and she's squinting, but I can tell she's been crying.

"Yes, I did have to, Yolanda."

"Fiona, I didn't do it. I want you to know that. I don't know how that answer sheet got into my schoolbag."

"I know you didn't."

"It was one of Natalie's crowd who stole the answers, wasn't it?" She looks away. "They're your friends now."

"Not the way you've been my friend."

"They're going to be angry at you."

"I don't care. They put it there. They put the answer sheet in your bag." She's stunned, doesn't know what to make of this. "I had to say something. It wasn't right."

She looks into my face, like she's searching for something she's not sure she's going to find anymore. "Well, I'm sure you would have done the same for anybody," she says. She sounds sad.

"It wasn't just anybody. It was you."

She looks down, then hikes her schoolbag higher on her shoulder. "Well, I owe you one," she says. "Thank you."

"You're welcome," I tell her and she turns to go. "Hey," I say, "want to come upstairs?"

She looks at me, confused. "What about your mom? She'll be home soon, won't she?"

"Yeah. So? I don't know whether my mom will come home or not. I don't know who I'll find in that apartment."

"She won't like finding me there."

I shrug, and that makes her smile.

"Okay," she says, as if that's all it takes to decide.

We head toward the building, and in a few steps, I take her hand. I need to know she's really with me. She squeezes my hand, and I hear something catch in her throat. I feel like I'm going to cry, too.

Upstairs, outside the apartment door, we can hear the TV. When I open it, my mother looks up. She's on the couch and her eyes are red, her face blotchy. Tissues are piled on the coffee table in front of her. She looks at me. Her gaze follows my arm down to the hand I'm holding. I try to read her face, but her puffy eyes don't tell me more than the obvious. She stands up and comes toward us. "I have to tell you something," she says, and for a second I'm not sure if the terrible news that's on her face is going to be about the Kennedy family or ours.

"What?" I say.

"President Kennedy … he …"

"I know, Mom. They told us in school."

"They did?" She looks shocked, trying to understand this, as if she's not sure this is something the teachers should have done, as if maybe this awful thing, this assault that feels so personal, is something that should have been left to parents to handle. She turns toward the sound of the television, uncertain what to do next.

I'm relieved that she's here, but still I'm not sure what has happened, where my father has gone. "Did Uncle Eddie talk to you? About this morning?" I ask.

"He told me," she says. And she holds her arms out to me. I let her hold me, 'cause she needs to, she needs to feel she can keep me from harm in this mess of a world. "Thank you, Fiona," she says. "Thank you." I pull away. I'm afraid I'll start crying.

"Yolanda is here," I say dumbly, as if she hadn't noticed.

"Yolanda," she says. That's all. Just Yolanda. And I watch her lean forward and give Yolanda sort of a hug. It's only the polite kind a diplomat might give you, but a hug just the same.

The three of us sit down so we can see the television, see if there's anyone who can tell us how this could have happened. "It's so sad," Mom says. "His poor family." On the screen, the anchorman looks so serious, so worried. I feel like I need to hold on to something solid, something that will stay in one piece no matter what. I take Yolanda's hand again. They're showing pictures of President Kennedy in a tuxedo with Jackie, sailing on a boat with her, playing by the water with his children. Then they show the hospital in Dallas. These pictures don't belong together. I look at the people crying on television and at my mother sitting on her couch natural as can be next to a girl with skin as dark as night. It's such a terrible day. And I don't know what will happen next. I don't know who will get the country to do all the good things the president wanted to do. And I don't know how my mom will manage on her own. But I know one thing: today the world is a different place.